"Just posing as my fiancée will be sufficient."

"Just falling into your bed, you mean." She was on him in a second, jabbing a finger into his chest, fire flashing from her angry eyes to his bewildered ones. "Is that how you intend to have me earn my salary, Romano?"

"Yes," he said. "I mean, no. I mean, I expect you to play the role you agreed to play."

"The deal was, I pretend to be your fiancée. And when I'm not pretending, I do the cooking. That's what I'm going to do. You got that?" He looked down at her. She looked enraged, and almost incredibly beautiful.

"Romano? Do we understand each other?"

What he understood was that he ached to make love to her. "Yes," he said, and he reached out, grasped her shoulders, put her aside and headed out the door.

SANDRA MARTON is an American author who used to tell stories to her dolls when she was a little girl. Today, readers around the world fall in love with her sexy, dynamic heroes and outspoken, independent heroines. Her books have topped bestseller lists and won many awards. Sandra loves dressing up for a night out with her husband as much as she loves putting on her hiking boots for a walk in a southwestern desert or a northeastern forest. You can write to her at P.O. Box 295, Storrs, Connecticut 06268 (please enclose SASE).

Note from the Editor: Some of you will have already met Joe Romano. He's the brother of Matt Romano, *The Sexiest Man Alive* (Harlequin Presents #2008). Many readers have got in touch to tell us how much they loved the story of Matt and how he won his lovely bride, Susannah, and asked if Joe might have a book of his own. Sandra Marton hasn't hesitated; with Matt happily married, Joe deserves his happy ending, too. How does it happen? With laughter, tears, a touch of lighthearted revenge and *plenty* of passion....

Sandra Marton

ROMANO'S REVENGE

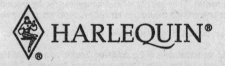

TORONTO • NEW YORK • LONDON
AMSTERDAM • PARIS • SYDNEY • HAMBURG
STOCKHOLM • ATHENS • TOKYO • MILAN • MADRID
PRAGUE • WARSAW • BUDAPEST • AUCKLAND

To the blonde who owns Joe's heart: thank you for
offering to share him with so many other women!

ISBN 0-373-12117-2

ROMANO'S REVENGE

First North American Publication 2000.

Visit us at www.eHarlequin.com

Printed in U.S.A.

CHAPTER ONE

THE women whose hearts had been broken by Joseph Romano, and the ones who yearned for the same fate, agreed that he was a black-haired, blue-eyed, sexy-as-hell, untamable, gorgeous hunk.

The old-line financial wizards who watched as Joe amassed millions on the San Francisco stock market said he was a cold-blooded, hot-tempered upstart. And they called him things a lot more graphic and less polite than "hunk."

Joe's grandmother, who'd adored him for the entirety of his thirty-two years, told anyone who would listen that her Joseph was handsome as a god, sweet-natured as an angel, and as smart as the you-know-what. Nonna had just enough of the Old Country left in her so that she wouldn't say the devil's name out loud any more than she'd say any of these things to Joe's face.

What she did tell him, as often as she could, was that he needed to eat his vegetables, get to bed on time, find a good Italian girl to marry and give her, Nonna, lots of beautiful, bright *bambinos*.

Joe loved his grandmother with all his heart. She and his brother, Matthew, were all the family he had left. And he tried to please her. He ate almost all his vegetables, except the ones no real man would ever eat. He went to bed on time, though his interest in being there had nothing to do with sleep and everything to do with the succession of beautiful women who passed through his busy life.

But marriage…well, a man didn't put his neck in that noose until he was ready.

Fortunately, Joe had never felt that ready. He didn't expect to, not for a long, long time.

An intelligent man, Joe never mentioned that to Nonna during the last-Friday-of-the-month suppers they both enjoyed whenever he was in town. Supper with her, and a bachelor party for one of the guys he played racquetball with, was why he'd flown back to San Francisco on a warm Friday in late May.

He'd been in New Orleans, checking out a small start-up company whose stock looked interesting. When the stacked redhead who'd been walking him through the firm's data leaned in close and said, in a sexy whisper, that she hoped he'd let her give him a more intimate tour of the French Quarter over the weekend, Joe had grinned and started to say he'd surely love that.

Then he'd remembered the bachelor party. More than that, he'd remembered that this was the last Friday of the month. Nonna had made a special point of reminding him that she expected to see him for dinner.

That was unusual. She never had to remind him because Joe never forgot. If anything, Nonna was always telling him that she didn't want him to feel locked into their once-a-month Fridays.

"You have other things you want to do, Joey," she'd say, "you do them."

Joe had hugged her and told her that he'd sooner break a date with the queen than miss a Friday with her.

It was true. Sometimes he figured his grandmother was the only reason he'd made it through childhood in one piece.

She'd taken him in a zillion times when he was a kid and his old man was looking to beat the crap out of him for some numbskull antic. She'd been a rock for him and Matt when their mother died. She'd never given up on him, even after he'd pretty much given up on himself. And, when he'd finally straightened himself out, joined the Navy and then the SEALs, been honorably discharged and completed his college education, Nonna had simply said she always knew he'd make something of himself.

So Joe had flown back to San Francisco that May night, climbed into his cherry-red Ferrari, stopped to buy a bouquet of spring flowers and the smooth-as-silk Chianti he and his grandmother liked. Then he drove to her clapboard house in North Beach. She'd lived in it as long as he could remember, despite the efforts of both Joe and Matt to convince her to leave it.

Nonna greeted him on the back porch.

"Joseph," she said, *"mio ragazzo."* She gave him a big hug. "Come inside, sweetheart, and *mangia."*

The hug and the smile were normal. The Italian was not.

His nonna had come to the States as a bride of sixteen. She spoke English with an accent but English was what she spoke, never her native Italian. Not unless she was nervous.

What was there for her to be nervous about? Joe frowned as he stepped inside the old-fashioned kitchen. Her health was excellent. He'd taken her to her doctor himself just a couple of weeks ago for her annual checkup. And he knew all was well with Matt and his wife, Susannah.

But Nonna was definitely behaving strangely. She was babbling—something else she never did, except when she was under some sort of stress—asking him about his trip but not giving him time to answer, telling him about her week without pausing for breath…

Maria Balducci.

The hair rose on the back of Joe's neck.

That was the last time he'd seen his grandmother in such a state, the night she'd tried to set him up with Maria Balducci, who lived up the street. He'd shown up for supper and Nonna had greeted him just like this, with an unaccustomed flurry of Italian and a table loaded not just with antipasto and lasagna or manicotti but everything imaginable. Veal piccata, shrimp scampi, steak pizzaola.

A table without so much as one vegetable on it, unless some crazed nutritionist had suddenly decided olives and garlic were the equal of cauliflower and, even worse, carrots.

A table that had looked, to his suspicious eyes, very much like it looked tonight.

Joe fought back the desire to flatten himself against the wall as he checked the room, but no one else was there. Certainly not Maria, and she would have been difficult to miss.

"Joseph." Nonna smiled a bright smile and bustled around the room. "Sit down, sit down, *mio ragazzo,* and have some antipasto. Prosciutto, just the way you like it. Provolone. Genoa, sliced thin as paper…"

"We're alone?"

Nonna clucked her tongue. "Of course. Do you think I have someone hidden in the broom closet?"

Anything was possible, Joe thought, but he didn't say so. Instead, he pulled out a chair and eased into it.

"No matchmaking," he said carefully. "Right?"

"Matchmaking?" Nonna laughed gaily. "Why would you even ask such a thing, Joseph, huh? You've told me how you feel. You aren't ready to marry a nice Italian girl, settle down and raise *una famiglia,* even though it's the one wish of my heart. So, why would I try and play matchmaker?"

Joe rolled his eyes. "Anybody ever tell you that you have a way with a phrase?"

"I have a way with food." His grandmother poked a finger at the platter of antipasto. *"Mangia."*

"Yeah. Sure." Obediently, he dug in, transferring what had to be a billion grams of fat and an equal number of calories to his plate.

"Good?" Nonna asked after a minute.

"Delicious." Joe reached for the basket heaped with garlic bread, hesitated, then snagged a piece and mentally added two miles to his morning run. "So, what's this all about?"

"What is what all about?"

He tried not to wince as his grandmother filled two water glasses with the elegant Chianti he'd brought and shoved one at him across the heavy white tablecloth.

"Come on, sweetheart. You made every dish I ever loved. You didn't even try and disguise carrots and cauliflower the way you always do in hopes you could slip them past me. And there are Italian words falling out of your mouth. Something's up."

"Non capisco," Nonna said.

Their eyes met, his the blue of the Mediterranean, hers as

dark as the hills of Sicily. Joe grinned, and his grandmother blushed.

"All right." Her voice was prim, her shrug small but eloquent. "Perhaps something is, as you say, 'up.' But it has nothing to do with matchmaking. Believe me, Joseph, I have given that up, completely."

Good manners, but mostly the knowledge that his nonna probably wasn't above boxing his ears, kept him from pointing out that he saw her cross herself as she rose from the table and went to the stove.

"I'll bet you have," he said pleasantly. Joe shoved his chair back from the table and folded his arms. "So, I can relax? Some eager female isn't going to come sailing through that doorway with a tray of cannoli in her arms?"

Nonna swung towards him, a pot of espresso in her hand. "Certainly not. I know full well that you prefer your dimbos to real women."

"Bimbos," Joe said, trying not to laugh. "And they aren't. They're just pretty young women who enjoy my company as much as I enjoy theirs."

Nonna sighed as she put the pot on the table. "Monday is your birthday," she said, taking cups and saucers from the cupboard.

The sudden change in conversation surprised him almost as much as the information.

"Is it?"

"Yes. You will be thirty-three."

"Now that you mention it, I guess I will." Joe smiled. "Of course. That's the reason for the feast." He grabbed her work-worn hand and brought it to his lips. "And here I thought you were up to something. Sweetheart, can you ever forgive me for being so suspicious?"

"I am your nonna. Of course, I forgive you." Nonna sat down and poured their coffee. "But, ah, this meal is not your gift."

"No?"

"No. Surely, a man's thirty-third birthday deserves more than food."

"Sweetheart." Joe kissed her hand again. "This isn't just food, it's ambrosia. I don't want you to spend your money on—"

"You and Matthew give me more money than I could ever use in this lifetime. Besides, I have spent nothing."

"Good."

"But I am giving you a gift, nevertheless." Nonna beamed at him over the rim of her cup. *"Giuseppe, mio ragazzo."*

Joe's eyes turned to slits. In a boardroom he'd have leaned towards the guy trying to scam him and said, bluntly, "Cut the crap." But this wasn't a boardroom, and this wasn't some smart-ass dude in a pin-striped suit. This was his grandma, and he loved her, so he sat up straight, folded his arms over his chest again, and fixed her with a steely look.

"Okay," he said, "let's have it."

Nonna looked pained. "Have what?"

"You're trying to con me."

"Con? What does this mean, this 'con'?"

"It means you want to convince me to do something I don't want to do."

"How can you think such a thing, Joseph?"

Joe arched one eyebrow. "How?"

"Yes." Nonna lifted her chin. "How?"

"Maria Balducci."

"Oh, not that nonsense again. Honestly, Joseph—"

"It was February," he said calmly, "and it was snowing. I showed up for supper and you plied me with steak pizzaola, shrimp scampi—"

"What is this 'plied you'? Did I grab that handsome nose of yours and drag you to the table?"

Joe plucked his napkin from his lap and dropped it on the table. "You know exactly what I'm talking about, Grandma."

"Grandma? I am your Nonna, and don't you forget it."

"You're the biggest matchmaker in North Beach," Joe said, shooting to his feet. "You dazzled me with goodies that night and then you brought out the big guns."

"I brought out espresso, as I recall."

"And Miss Italy 1943."

Nonna stood up, too. "Signora Balducci was your age, Joseph."

"She was dressed all in black."

"She is a widow."

"She had one giant eyebrow that stretched across her forehead."

He saw his grandmother's mouth twitch. "It was two eyebrows that merely needed plucking."

"How about that long hair growing out of the mole on her chin?" Joe's mouth also twitched, but he wasn't going to laugh, not yet. "I suppose that could be plucked, too?"

"You see? That's your problem, Joseph. There is no way to please you. That time I introduced you to Anna Carbone—"

"The teenybopper at that festival you dragged me to last summer?"

"I did not 'drag' you," Nonna said with dignity. "I merely said I needed you to drive me there. It was coincidence that Anna should have been waiting for me. And she was not a teeny-banger."

"Bopper. Yes, she was. It's a miracle she didn't still have braces on her teeth."

"She was twenty. But I did not argue when you said she was too young, did I?"

"No," Joe said coolly, "no, you didn't. You just waited awhile and found Miss Eyebrow."

Nonna's lips twitched again. "Actually, I'd never noticed the eyebrows. Not until that night, in this kitchen. "

"Uh-huh. When the *signora* just happened to arrive at the door with dessert."

"And the mole."

Joe and his grandmother looked at each other and smiled. He sighed, took her in his arms, and pressed a kiss to her forehead.

"Okay," he said, "let's have it."

"Have what?"

"I want to know what 'gift' you're giving me for my birthday, and why you're buttering up me up beforehand." He looked over her head, at the door. "Is my dessert arriving by female express?"

Nonna made a face. She bustled past him, opened the freezer and took out a bowl. "*Gelato*. Just so you know that your dessert is not climbing the porch steps."

Joe smiled and sat down again. "Homemade ice cream. Nonna, you're going to spoil me."

Nonna smiled. She waited until he'd spooned up a mouthful. "Good?"

"Wonderful. The best you ever made."

Her smile tilted slyly. "Good. But I didn't make it."

Joe looked up. "You must have. Not even Carbone's has *gelato* this delicious."

"You're right. Signor Carbone would kill for this recipe."

"Well," Joe said, "if you didn't get it at Carbone's and you didn't make it, who…" The words caught in his throat. Slowly, he put down his spoon and looked at his grandmother. "All right," he said grimly. "Let's have it. And don't embarrass either of us by giving me that wide-eyed, I-don't-know-what-you're-talking-about look."

Nonna folded her hands on the white tablecloth.

"I worry about you, Joseph."

Despite what she'd said before, here it was. They were going to go over the same old thing again.

"Nonna," Joe said patiently, "we've been all through this. I'm not lonely. I don't want a wife. I'm happy with my life, just the way it is."

"You remember once, I asked you who sews the buttons on your shirts, huh? Who irons them?"

"And I told you," Joe said briskly. "The guy at the laundry. And he does a great job."

"Yes. And you told me your house is cleaned by a cleaning service."

"That's right. The same service I wish you'd let me send here, so you don't have to bother—"

"I prefer to clean my own house," Nonna said primly. She leaned forward. "But, Joseph, who cooks your meals?"

Joe sighed. "I told you that the last time around, too. I don't eat home much. And when I do, there are all these terrific little take-out places a couple of blocks away... What?''

Nonna was smiling, and something about the smile made him want to get out of the chair and run for his life.

"I have accepted that perhaps you will never be ready to marry, Joseph, and that you are happy to let strangers iron your shirts and clean your home. But I have never stopped worrying about your meals."

"There's no reason to worry, sweetheart. I eat just fine."

"I will not worry from now on." His grandmother dug deep into the pocket of her apron. "Happy birthday, Joey," she said, and thrust a folded piece of paper at him.

Joe took it and frowned. "What is this?"

"Your birthday gift." His grandmother was beaming, her eyes bright with joy. "Open it."

He did. Then he looked up. "I don't understand. This is just a name."

"*Sì.* It is a name. Luciana Bari."

The vowels and consonants rolled off his grandmother's tongue. Joe's jaw tightened.

"And just who in hell is Luciana Bari?"

"Do not curse, Joseph."

"And don't you try and change the subject. We just spent an hour talking about teenyboppers, overage widows and your sneaky attempts to marry me off. If you for one minute think you can get away with this—"

Oh, damn. His grandmother's eyes filled with tears. Joe grabbed her hand.

"Nonna. Sweetheart, I didn't mean to call you sneaky. But after all we discussed, for you to imagine I'd be pleased by—"

"Luciana Bari isn't a woman," Nonna said. "She is a cook."

A tear rolled down her cheek. Joe took out his handkerchief and gave it to her. "A cook?"

"Yes. A talented one." Nonna dabbed at her eyes. "She made the *gelato* and even you admit it was delicious."

Joe sat back. Trapped! Warning bells began to sound in his head; lights flickered and flashed before his eyes.

"Well," he said slowly, "yeah. It was. I mean, it is. But
what does this Luciana Bari have to do with me?"

"She is your gift, Joseph. " Nonna's lip trembled. "My gift
to you. And I am saddened that you would think I was trying
to, as you say, 'con' you."

Dammit, she was. Joe knew she was—but her lip was still
trembling and her eyes were still glittering. And, to be honest,
the lingering taste of the *gelato* was still in his mouth.

"My gift," he said carefully. "So, what does that mean,
exactly? Is this Luciana Bari going to cook me a birthday
meal?"

Nonna laughed gaily. "One meal," she said, waving her
hand. "What good would that be? I would still worry that you
were not eating right. No, Joey. Signorina Bari is going to
work for you."

"Work for me?" Joe got to his feet. "Now, wait just a
minute—"

"She will cost you very little."

"She will cost *me?*" His eyes narrowed. His grandmother
had reduced him to playing the role of a not terribly smart
parrot. "Let me get this straight. You give me a cook as a gift,
and I get to pay?"

"Of course." Nonna stood up. "You wouldn't want me to
spend my money on your cook's salary, would you?"

Joe's eyes got even narrower. There was something wrong
with her logic. With this entire thing, for that matter...

"What if I say no?"

"Well," Nonna said, and sighed, "in that case, I suppose
I'll have to phone Signorina Bari and tell her she has no job.
It will be difficult, because she needs one so badly." She
turned away and began clearing the table. "She has debts, you
see."

"Debts," Joe repeated. It was parrot-time again. "She has
debts?"

"Yes. The poor woman has not been here long. Just a little
while and—"

"She's from the Old Country?"

Nonna squirted dishwashing detergent into the sink and turned on the hot water.

"The poor soul only came here five, six months ago. She knows nothing of our ways. As for money, well, you know how expensive it is in this city, Joseph, especially for someone new. And she is not young, which makes it even more difficult to start over."

Joe sank down in the chair, turned his eyes to the ceiling and huffed out a breath. A little old immigrant lady, probably with no more than a dozen words of English, alone and adrift in the complex seas of San Francisco...

"Not to worry, Joseph." Nonna cast a sad smile over her shoulder. "I'll tell her I made a mistake, offering her a job with you. I'm sure she can convince her landlord to permit her to stay on in her apartment another month. Not even he would be so cruel as to put her out on the street."

"Her landlord," Joe muttered, and shook his head.

"Yes. He wants her out by Monday, so she was thrilled when I said she could have that extra room in your house."

Joe blinked. "Now wait just a minute—"

"Hand me that pot, would you? The one on the back burner."

Slowly, like a man holding an impossibly heavy weight on his shoulders, Joe got to his feet, handed his grandmother the pot and reached for a dish towel.

"Ah, Joseph, just look at you." Nonna put her hand on his. "I've taken the smile from your handsome face."

"Yeah," he said gruffly. "Well, I hate to think of some little old lady out on the street."

"That's because you have a kind heart." Nonna sighed. "But, truly, this is not your problem. I was wrong to tell the *signorina* you would employ her, I know that now. Not to worry, *bambino*. We have so many wonderful things here in America. Soup kitchens. Welfare offices—"

"I suppose I could let her work for me for a little while," Joe said slowly.

He'd expected his grandmother to say it wasn't necessary, to argue just a little. Instead she swung towards him, beaming.

"You are a good boy, Joseph! I knew you would do this for her."

"I'm doing it for you. And I won't do it for long."

"No. Certainly not." Nonna's smile broadened. "Two months, three—"

"Two weeks," Joe corrected. "Three, max. By then, I'll expect the *signora* to have found herself a real job and a real place to live."

"*Signorina.*" Nonna made a face. "Not that it matters," she said, plunging her hands into the soapy water. "The poor woman."

"What?" Joe frowned. "Is there something else I should know about her?"

"Honesty compels me to point out that the *signorina* is not at all attractive."

Joe thought back to the widow and that eyebrow.

"No?"

"No. The *signorina* is very pale. And very thin. She is shapeless, like a boy." Nonna made curving motions over her own ample bosom. "She has no—no—"

"I get the message," Joe said quickly. He arched an eyebrow. "You sure she's Italian?"

Nonna chuckled. "Of course. She learned to cook in *Fiorenze.*" Her smile dimmed and she heaved a huge sigh as she opened the drain, then wiped her hands on her apron. "She is, how do you say, over the hill. Not young, Joseph. Not young."

A pasty-faced, skinny crone who spoke no English. Talk about good deeds... Joe sighed. People had told him he was born to be hung, but at this rate he'd end up in heaven, after all.

"Well," he said kindly, "as long as she can cook, that's okay."

Nonna turned and faced him. "And, just in case you are still worried, I can assure you that she will not bother you with her attentions. This, I promise."

And a good thing, too, Joe thought. The last thing he needed was to find himself fending off an old lady.

"I know how the women fall all over you, Joey."

"Uh, yeah." He tried for a modest smile. "Some of them seem to, I guess."

"But the *signorina* will not do so."

"Yeah, well, considering her age…"

"She does not like men."

"Fine."

"No, Joseph. What I mean is…" His grandmother leaned closer. "She does not like men."

The words dripped with significance. Joe stared at her.

"You mean…?" No. He couldn't say the word, not to his nonna. "You mean," he finished inanely, "she *really* doesn't like men?"

"Exactly." Nonna put her hands on her hips. "You see? It's perfect. She will never be a bother to you, nor you to her. And I can go to my grave in peace, knowing you are eating properly."

Joseph's eyes narrowed. "You're not going anywhere, you old reprobate. Not for a very long time."

"I am not whatever it is you call me," Nonna said sweetly. "I am simply a doting grandmother, giving her favorite grandson a gift."

"Some gift," Joe said, but he smiled, tossed the towel aside and put his arms around her waist. "You're precisely what I called you, which is why I'd never play poker with you, or sit across from you at a boardroom table."

"Flatterer." Nonna batted her lashes and smiled up at him. "You're much too clever for an old lady like me."

"Yeah," Joe said, and grinned, "I'll bet."

"Now," Nonna said briskly, "how about more espresso?"

Joe shook his head. "I wish I could, sweetheart, but I'm going to have to run."

"So soon?"

"I have an appointment. One of the guys I play racquetball with is…" Getting married, he'd almost said, but the last thing he wanted to do was bring up that subject again. "He's having a party at his place on Nob Hill. I promised I'd be there."

"Ah." Nonna smiled, framed Joe's face in her hands, drew it down to her and kissed him on each cheek. "How nice.

Would you like to take along some food? I can put a little of everything into some Tupperware…''

"No," Joe said quickly, "uh, really, it would just upset the, uh, the caterer."

"Oh. Of course. I didn't think of that." Nonna stuffed her hands into her apron pockets. "Well, you have a good time, Joey."

"I'll try." Joe reached for his suit jacket. He put his arm around his grandmother and they walked together to the door. "I love you, Nonna."

"And I love you." Nonna lifted her face for his kiss. "Remember now. Your new cook will be at your door tomorrow morning, bright and early."

"Oh. Oh, yeah." For a minute there he'd almost forgotten that he'd agreed to this crazy plan. Well, it wouldn't kill him to let the woman cook a few meals for him before he found her another job. The city had to be full of people who'd want the services of a talented Italian cook, even if she was old, ugly, and a lesbian. "I'm looking forward to meeting her. What was her name again?"

"Luciana. Luciana Bari."

"Right. Luciana Bari, formerly of Florence, Italy." He grinned as he stepped onto the porch. "She sounds perfect."

"She *is* perfect," Nonna Romano said, and meant it.

In a house on Nob Hill, Lucinda Barry, of the Boston Barrys, the we-came-over-on-the-*Mayflower* Barrys, the oh-boy, we-are-broke Barrys…

Lucinda Barry, who had moved from the east coast to the west and sworn off men forever after her fiancé had dumped her for a brainless twit with money…

Lucinda Barry, whose landlord had just tossed her out for nonpayment of rent, who'd taken a quick course in desperation cooking from Chef Florenze at the San Francisco School of Culinary Arts, who was to start her very first job ever tomorrow as a cook for a sensitive, charming, undoubtedly gay gentleman she hoped would be too kind to notice that pretty much all she could do right was boil water and, amazingly enough, whip up terrific *gelato*...

That Lucinda Barry stood in the marble-and-gold powder room of the house on Nob Hill, eyed herself in the mirror and wondered why Fate should have done this to her.

"I can't do it," Lucinda whispered to her blond, green-eyed reflection.

Of course you can, her reflection said briskly. *You don't have a choice.*

The girl hired to jump out of the cake had come down with food poisoning.

"Not from our food," Chef Florenze had said coldly as the ambulance took the writhing young woman away. Then he'd frowned, scanned the little crowd of would-be culinary school graduates gathered around him for the night of cooking that would be their final exam, and pointed a stubby finger at Lucinda. "You," he'd roared, and when Lucinda stepped back in horror, saying no, no, she was a cook, not a stripper—when she did, the chef smiled unpleasantly and said she wasn't a cook, either, not until he handed over her graduation certificate...

"Ms. Barry!"

Lucinda jumped at the knock on the door.

"Ms. Barry," the chef demanded, "what on earth is taking you so long?"

Lucinda straightened her shoulders and looked at herself in the mirror.

How tough could it be to trade her white chef's hat, jacket and trousers for a gilded tiara, a pair of demitasse cups and a thong, and then jump out of a cardboard cake?

"Not as tough as being broke, jobless and homeless," Lucinda muttered grimly, and set about the business of transforming herself from a cook into a cookie.

CHAPTER TWO

OKAY. Okay, so the transformation wasn't going to be easy, but then, she hadn't expected it to be.

Cinderella had done it with the help of a fairy godmother.

Lucinda looked at the cake costume and shuddered. All she had to rely upon were spangles, sequins and Lycra.

Solemnly, she took off her chef's hat and laid it aside. She unbuttoned her spotless white jacket, took it off, rebuttoned it, folded it carefully and put it next to the hat. Her trousers went next. Zipped, folded neatly on the crease, she added them to the sad little collection.

Then she took a deep breath, stepped into the bikini bottom and yanked it up over her hips.

It didn't fit. The thong didn't fit! Hope rushed through her veins. She couldn't be expected to jump out of a cake in her chef's outfit. If the costume didn't fit...

Oh, hell.

Lucinda moaned softly as she looked at herself in the mirror.

Of course the thong didn't fit. How could it, when she'd tried pulling it on over her white cotton underpants?

She almost laughed. What a sight she was! Wire-rimmed glasses. No makeup. Hair pulled severely back from her face. A utilitarian, white cotton bra, the white cotton panties... And, over the panties, the thong.

She looked like a cross between Mary Poppins and Madonna.

The desire to laugh slipped away. Lucinda gritted her teeth, shucked off both the thong and the panties, then put the thong on again.

Goodbye, Mary Poppins.

The view wasn't so bad from the front. Well, it wasn't good. Still, it covered what had to be covered. But from the back...

20

Her face went from pink to red as she twisted and turned and peered at herself in the mirror. The thong went up. It went straight up. It just went up there and disappeared.

"Ms. Barry!"

The door jumped under the pounding of Chef Florenze's fist. Lucinda jumped, too.

"Ms. Barry, do you hear me?"

How could she not hear him, she thought bitterly. He was shouting. He had to, she supposed, to make himself heard over the rock and roll music blaring from the ballroom.

Okay, she couldn't expect a bunch of men at a bachelor party to be listening to Mozart but for heaven's sake, did they have to listen to some idiot singing that he'd been born to be wild?

Whatever had happened to Chopin?

"You have five minutes, Ms. Barry!"

Five minutes.

Lucinda swung towards the mirror and stared at herself again. The cotton bra did nothing for the thong. Or maybe it was the thong that did nothing for the bra, she thought, and bit down on her lip.

"This is not funny," she told herself severely.

And it wasn't. The desire to laugh had nothing to do with seeing anything even slightly humorous in the situation. She was verging on hysteria. She remembered the first time it had happened, that out-of-place, overwhelming bark of laughter. It had been the day after her father's funeral when his attorney had gently told the truth to her mother, and to her...

Lucinda lifted her chin.

"Just do it," she said grimly, and she stripped off the cotton bra, put on the spangled demitasse cups, and faced herself in the mirror again.

It was her reflection that seemed to want to laugh this time. Who are you kidding? it seemed to say.

Never mind the silly excuse for a bra and the thong. She looked about as sexy as a scarecrow.

Any self-respecting male would take one look and beg her to jump back *into* the cake.

Lucinda frowned. Well, so what? Even if—*if*—she did this, whether she looked sexy doing it or not wasn't her problem. Popping out of the cake was her problem, but as she'd learned over the past two years, desperation could make you do a lot of things. Like waitressing, and flipping hamburgers. Like admitting that being descended from Cotton Mather didn't mean scratch compared to being descended from a father who'd left behind a house that was mortgaged to the hilt, a defeated wife and a disappointed mistress.

The mistress had found a new man. The wife—Lucinda's mother—had found a new husband.

And Lucinda was finding a new life.

At least, that was the plan. It was why she'd put three thousand miles between herself and Boston, come to a city where nobody's eyebrows would lift when they heard the name "Barry," and nobody would say, with a little smirk, "Why, Lucinda, however are you, dear?" when what they really meant was, "Oh, Lucinda, how nice to see that the mighty have fallen."

Lucinda's shoulders straightened. It had been a silly life, anyway. The theater. The opera. Charity balls, and endless parties for the needy cause of the moment. Well, she was her own needy cause now. But she'd be a productive citizen, once she had her cooking school certificate in hand.

Once she had that job, tomorrow.

And there'd be no job, without that certificate.

Lucinda leaned forward, palms flat on the marble top of the vanity, and stared unflinchingly into the mirror. Oh, yes, she thought wryly. Looking like this, she'd definitely be a big hit at that stag party.

One by one, she took the pins from her chignon and shook out her hair. Unbound, the straight-as-sticks ash-blond tresses fell heavily to her shoulders.

That was better, she thought dispassionately.

Now for the glasses. She usually wore contacts but she'd dropped one getting ready to leave the apartment this evening, and there hadn't been enough time to crawl around on her hands and knees and search for it. She wouldn't be able to see that well without the glasses but then, she was going to be the cake decoration, not the decorator.

Lucinda swallowed hard as she set them on the sink. Her reflection was wavy around the edges. Actually, wavy around the edges was an excellent description of how she felt. Her belly had knotted into one gigantic ball that had lodged itself somewhere between her throat and her all-too-visible navel.

Was she really going to be the first Barry female ever to emerge, naked, from the center of a giant cake?

A six-layer white cake, swirled with milk-chocolate frosting and decorated with marzipan hearts and stars. She'd applied them herself, just this afternoon…

Lucinda gave herself a little shake. What did it matter who'd applied what to the damned thing? Besides, Chef Florenze had made it clear she would not actually leap through the real cake. Why ruin the best part of a dozen eggs, two pounds of butter, and all that confectioner's sugar?

"It will be a cardboard cake," he'd said while she'd gawked at him. "You will pop from it cleanly."

Perhaps it was his incredible assumption that she'd even consider doing such a thing. Perhaps it was his solemn assurance that she wouldn't have to contend with leaping through the butter-cream frosting. Whichever, a wild image had bloomed in Lucinda's head. She'd pictured herself bursting from the top of a cardboard cake wearing the tiara, the thong, the barely-there excuse for a bra, and a jack-in-the-box mask.

The first semi-crazed snort of amusement had burst from her throat. The chef, naturally enough, had misunderstood.

"Ah," he'd said with a beaming smile, "I am delighted to see that this little assignment is to your liking, Ms. Barry. I had, if only for a moment, feared you might, ah, might not be pleased with it."

"Pleased?" Lucinda had repeated, the urge to laugh buried under the stronger urge to connect her fist with Chef Florenze's chubby triple chins. "*Pleased* with being told you want me to display myself, naked, to a mob of howling hyenas?" She'd looked down at the small white box that held the costume he wanted her to wear and shoved it back at him. "Have you lost your mind?"

"Ms. Barry. I have explained the situation. The actress hired for the occasion—"

"Actress," Lucinda said, and gave another snort, though not of amusement.

"She has fallen ill. And you must take her place. I've told you that three times."

"And I've told you that I'm here to cook, not to—to entertain a bunch of degenerates."

The chef drew himself up. "Degenerates, indeed," he said coldly. "These men are drawn from the finest families in San Francisco. They are captains of industry."

"They are drunk," Lucinda replied, even more coldly.

"They're celebrating. And a girl popping out of a cake is part of the celebration."

"Call a modeling agency. Call wherever it is you hired that 'actress' and hire another." Lucinda folded her arms and looked the chef in the eye. "I'm not doing it."

Florenze waved a pudgy hand at the wall clock. "It's almost ten at night. The agency is closed."

"A pity."

"Do you recall culinary lesson three? How to improvise when the soufflé falls?"

"What has that to do with this?"

"I am improvising, Ms. Barry. I am making do with the materials at hand."

Lucinda's eyes narrowed. "I am neither an egg white nor a bar of bitter chocolate, Chef Florenze."

The chef smiled thinly. "Look around you. Go on, look. What do you see?"

"The kitchen in which I'm supposed to be working."

"What you see," he said impatiently, "are six students. Three men, three women, yourself included."

"So?"

"So," the chef purred, "I suspect we can agree that our guests would be less than delighted if Mr. Purvis, Mr. Rand or Mr. Jensen leaped from a cake tonight, hmm?"

Lucinda said nothing.

"Can we agree, too, that the venerable Miss Robinson would surely get hurt trying to extricate herself from anything other than an armchair? And that Mrs. Selwyn would never fit inside a cake unless it had the dimensions of Cheops' pyramid?"

"What you're asking me to do is a barbaric, sexist, disgusting custom."

"So are half the things done on this planet, but we are not anthropologists, we are caterers." The chef moved closer. "Our catering contract calls for roast beef, barbecued pork, filet of sole almondine, assorted salads and breads, coffee, beverages—and a giant cardboard cake that contains a young lady. Is that clear?"

"A very strange contract for a catering firm, if you ask me."

"I'm not asking you for legal advice, Ms. Barry. I am telling you that you will put on that costume and do what must be done."

"I paid my tuition to be taught to cook."

The chef had smiled slyly at that, and Lucinda had, for the first time, felt the ground slip, ever so slightly, beneath her feet.

"Which you have not learned to do very well."

He was right, but what did that have to do with anything? "I attended the specified number of classes," she'd said coolly. "I passed all the exams. I earned my certificate."

The chef, damn him, had laughed.

"All your exams but the last," he'd said. "And you won't get your certificate, if you fail tonight's test."

Meaning, Lucinda thought as she looked into the mirror, meaning, she would have to pop out of that miserable cardboard creation or walk away from Chef Florenze's culinary school without the piece of paper she so desperately needed.

With it, she'd be a woman with a skill. She could parlay the cook's job the school had lined up for her into a job as a sous-chef at a restaurant, and go from that into being a full-fledged chef with her own restaurant someday, or her own catering firm…

Without it, she'd be back to waitressing.

"That's blackmail," Lucinda had protested, and Chef Florenze had shown his teeth beneath his skinny excuse of a mustache and said yes, yes, it was, and she was welcome to try and prove any of this conversation had taken place because it hadn't.

"Just think of this as your fifteen minutes of fame," he'd purred. "Your once-in-a-lifetime moment in the sun—"

"Just give me the miserable costume and shut up," Lucinda had snapped, and startled the both of them.

And now, here she stood. In the wings, as it were, dressed in little more than a handkerchief and two halves of a diaphanous, spangled eggshell.

"Lucinda," she said aloud, "are you insane?"

She had to be, even to have contemplated doing this thing.

"Ridiculous," she said, and quickly gathered her hair at the base of her neck.

The audacity of Chef Florenze. The nerve! How dare he do this to her? She was a Barry, and Barrys had stood firm on their principles for more than three hundred years. Well, except for her father, of course. But other Barrys had always Done The Right Thing. Hepzibah Barry had been burned alive in Salem, rather than say she was a witch. Could she, Lucinda Barry, do any less in the face of misfortune?

"Lucinda?" The doorknob rattled. "Lucinda, open this door at once!"

The voice was faint but unmistakable. Miss Robinson was demanding entry.

Oh, Lord. Miss Robinson. Eighty years old, at least. Tiny, ramrod-straight Miss Robinson, with her permed silver hair, her black dresses buttoned to the throat and wrist, her parchment-paper skin...

"Lucinda! Open the door and let me in."

Lucinda undid the lock and cracked the door an inch. "Miss Robinson." She took a breath. "I'm, uh, I'm kind of busy in here. If you need to use the, uh, if you need to use the facilities, I'm afraid you'll have to—"

"I've come to talk to you. Stop babbling and let me inside."

Lucinda grabbed a guest towel from the vanity, clutched it to her bosom and opened the door just wide enough to let the old woman enter.

"Now," Miss Robinson said briskly, "why are you hiding in here? What is this nonsense about?"

Lucinda's brows arched. "Miss Robinson," she said politely, "I appreciate your concern, but this, ah, this situation has nothing to do with—"

"Why are you stumbling all over your words? And why are you holding on to that towel as if it were the last life jacket on the *Titanic?*"

"Well—well, because what I'm wearing is—is—" Lucinda frowned, took a deep breath and dropped the towel to the tile floor. "This is why," she said coolly. "As you can see, I'm not exactly dressed for company."

The expression on the old woman's face didn't change as she looked Lucinda up, then down, then up again.

"Skimpy," she said at last.

Lucinda managed a tight smile. "Indeed."

"But I've seen bathing suits as revealing on the beach." Miss Robinson shook her head. "The things young women wear nowadays…"

"Yes, well, not *this* young woman!" Lucinda swung back towards the mirror and plucked a bobby pin from the counter. "Would you believe that Chef Florenze actually expects me to wear this thing? To scrunch down under a serving cart and…" Her eyes met the older woman's in the mirror. "Never mind. It doesn't bear repeating. Suffice it to say, I'm not going to do it."

"Don't be ridiculous," Miss Robinson said irritably. She reached out and snatched the pins from Lucinda's hair as fast as Lucinda anchored them. "Of course, you'll do it."

"Miss Robinson," Lucinda said patiently, "you have no idea what the chef wants."

"He wants you to jump out of a cardboard cake so those silly boys in the ballroom can clap their hands, whistle like banshees and generally make asses of themselves."

Lucinda stared at the other woman in the mirror. Then she turned and stared at her some more.

"He told you?"

"He told everyone. He also told us you've locked yourself in here and refuse to emerge."

"Did he mention that he's threatened to blackmail me? That he won't give me my certificate if I don't cooperate?" Lucinda smiled tightly. "Well, that nasty little man is in for a surprise. He doesn't believe I'll bring charges against him, but I will. I'll take him to court. I'll sue. I'll go to the papers... What?"

"That 'nasty little man' has expanded the scope of his ultimatum. Either you do as he's ordered, or none of us will get our certificates."

"But—but he can't do that."

Mrs. Robinson stamped her foot. "Don't be so naive, Lucinda! Of course he can do it. He can do whatever he likes. And you can do whatever you like about fighting him, but by the time the problem's resolved, it will be too late."

"That's not so," Lucinda said stubbornly. "The chef will still have to hand over those certificates, whether it's tonight or next week or next month."

"Yes, but that will be too late for Mr. Purvis, who's already accepted a restaurant position, and for the Rand lad. Did you know he took a student loan to pay for this course?" Miss Robinson put her bony hands on her hips. "And definitely too late for me. A woman my age has little time to spare."

"Don't be silly. Why, you don't look a day over—"

"Don't patronize me, girl."

"I'm not, I just..." Lucinda huffed out a breath. "Miss Robinson, now you're the one who's trying blackmail!"

"It's reality, not blackmail. Is your pride so important you'd ruin things for the rest of us?"

"Pride has nothing to do with this. It's a matter of principle."

The old lady snorted. "Better to concern yourself with the sort of principal that pays bills." Her eyes fixed on Lucinda's face. "How much has that horrid little man offered to pay you?"

"Pay me?"

"For this cake-jumping business."

"Why—why, nothing. He said he wouldn't give me my certificate unless—"

"Tell him you'll do it for two hundred dollars."

Lucinda stared at the old woman. "There's not a way in the world I'd do this, not even for—"

"Three hundred, then." Miss Robinson lifted a brow. "Unless, of course, you don't need money any more than you need that job you told us about, the one you're *supposed* to start tomorrow morning."

Lucinda glared at Miss Robinson. Old people were supposed to be sweet-natured and kindhearted but this one looked as if she had the disposition of an alligator.

"Of course I need money," she said coldly. "And the job, too."

"Then let down your hair, put on some lipstick, and get this over with." A sudden, wicked glint lit the old lady's eyes. "At least, you'll have a bra to wear. I didn't, back in the days when I was a showgirl with the Folies Bergère."

Lucinda's jaw dropped. "When you..."

"Indeed. When the heating system went on the blink at the Folies, the entire audience could tell you were cold."

Miss Robinson winked and turned around. The door swung shut after her. Lucinda hesitated. Then she turned and met her own gaze in the mirror.

The Folies Bergére? She tried to imagine Miss Robinson strutting down a runway dressed in feathers and a smile. Dressed in lots less than this costume, that was for sure.

Okay. So, maybe she had seen swimsuits as revealing on the beach. She'd never worn one, of course; she'd never worn anything more showy than the black tank suit she'd worn when she was a student at the Stafford School.

Only a madwoman would go from that stretched-out nylon tank to this bit of spangles and Lycra.

She turned, poked one shoulder towards the mirror.

Besides, even if she were to agree to do this thing—not that she would, but it didn't hurt to pretend—if she did, the men attending the bachelor party would be sorely disappointed.

Lucinda backed up a little, put on her glasses and took a better look.

Her neck was long, her shoulders too bony, her breasts too small.

She turned a little more, narrowed her eyes and took another look.

Well, small, yes. But rounded, and high. She sucked in her breath. Definitely, rounded and high. Her tummy was flat, her waist narrow. That was good. Her hips weren't much but her backside seemed okay. From what she'd heard, men liked women to have okay backsides. Long legs, too. And hers were surely that. She'd always had trouble buying panty hose that was long enough without being saggy and baggy on top…

What was she thinking? She'd never go out there. Never.

Do you want that job, Lucinda?

Oh, Lord. Yes. Yes, she did. She'd interviewed for it with a sweet old woman. A Mrs. Romano, who'd seemed undeterred by her inexperience.

"Never mind," Mrs. Romano had said reassuringly. "My grandson won't be picky, Luciana."

"It's Lucinda," Lucinda had said politely. "He won't be?"

"No. You see, he needs you."

"Needs me? I don't understand."

"He is a busy man. Always going here and there. *Molto importante,* yes? But he lacks something in his life."

"A cook?" Lucinda had said helpfully.

"Exactly. He doesn't eat right. He doesn't touch his vegetables."

"Vegetables." That was good. She could prepare green salads with the best of them.

"You will love working for him, Luciana."

"Lucinda."

"Of course. Lucinda. He's very easygoing. Charming, and gentle." Mrs. Romano had clasped her hands and sighed. "He is caring. And sensitive. My Joseph is the most sensitive man in all of San Francisco."

Gay, was what she'd meant. Lucinda had understood the code word, and the job had become even more appealing. A wealthy gay man who traveled a lot would be easy to work for. Gay men abounded in San Francisco, and the ones Lucinda had met were invariably low-key, gentle, and kind.

Kind enough to hire her, if the chef flunked her out of the cooking school?

"No way," Lucinda said, and knew the time for excuses was long gone.

She kept Miss Robinson firmly in mind as she let down her hair and ran her hands through it until it had the tousled look she'd noticed in magazine ads. She had no lipstick; she rarely used makeup. But there was a little cosmetics bag in the costume box. Inside, she found eye shadow. Eyeliner. Lucinda used them all, then bit her lips to pinken them. Finally, she put on the tiara and squinted at herself in the mirror.

Something was missing, but what? Her hair was okay. The glasses were gone. The costume fit as well as it was going to fit. Still, there was more. She'd forgotten something...

She jumped as a fist pounded against the closed door. "Well, Ms. Barry?" Chef Florenze boomed. "Are you going to grace us with your presence?"

Lucinda put her hand to her heart, as if to keep it from bounding out of her chest. Then, before she could change her mind, she unlocked the door and marched out.

"Very sensible of you, Miss Barry," the chef said with an unctuous smile.

Lucinda marched up to him. "Three hundred bucks, or I don't move from this spot."

"Don't be ridiculous."

"Three hundred."

Florenze's narrow mustache twitched. "Two."

"Two-fifty."

"Listen here, young woman—" Something in her eyes must have convinced him that she meant it. "Two-fifty," he said, "and snap to it."

"That's the spirit," she heard Miss Robinson say as she

strode to the serving cart that held the cardboard cake and climbed under it.

Her stomach gave a dangerous lurch. So did the cart. The rubber wheels squealed as she, and it, were pushed across the floor. Doors slammed against walls as they were opened. She heard the sounds of music and male laughter, and then the pounding of a chord—C major, she thought dispassionately—on a piano.

"Gentlemen," a deep voice cried, "to Arnie and his loss of freedom!"

"To Arnie," other male voices chorused.

"Now, Ms. Barry," Chef Florenze hissed, and Lucinda took a breath and burst through the top of the cake, arms extended gracefully above her head, just as if she were back in Boston, diving not up into the noise and the light but down, down, down into the glassy depths of a warm, blue pool.

But it wasn't a pool, it was a stage, and she hadn't burst free of the cardboard cake. She'd gotten tangled in it. And while she was still blinking and fighting furiously to extricate herself from the horrible chunks of cardboard, two things happened, almost simultaneously.

The first was that she realized that the "something" she'd forgotten were her low-heeled, sensible white shoes. They were still on her feet.

The other was that a man, a blur of muscles and blue eyes and black hair, had come to her rescue.

"Just put your arms around my neck, honey, and hang on."

"I am not your honey," Lucinda said. "And I don't need your help!"

She slapped at his hands as he reached for her but his arms closed around her, anyway. The crowd cheered as he hoisted her into his arms.

"Go for it, Joe," somebody yelled, and the man grinned, right into her eyes.

"Love those shoes," he purred, and when the crowd cheered again, he bent his head, covered her mouth with his, and kissed her.

CHAPTER THREE

JOE awoke to the sort of foggy, gray morning that gave San Francisco a bad name, a pounding headache—and the nagging sense that he'd made an ass of himself the night before.

Carefully, he eased his shoulders up against the headboard of his king-size bed. If he moved slowly enough, maybe his head wouldn't separate from his shoulders the way it was threatening to do.

The fog coiling around the bedroom windows was okay. Actually, it was fine. He was pretty sure that even a single ray of sunlight would have been enough to trigger the incipient implosion of his skull.

The pain would ease up eventually, he knew, but the feeling that he'd done something incredibly stupid might not. That was different. The feeling just wouldn't go away.

What? What could he have...

"Oh, hell."

He groaned, closed his eyes and slid down against the pillows.

Damned right, he'd made an ass of himself.

How else to describe a man who'd kissed the blond babe who'd come out of that cake?

He knew he'd never hear the end of it, especially since he'd always made it a point to distance himself from that kind of silliness. All right, so guys did it all the time. He'd been at a dozen bachelor bashes and there was almost always some idiot who leaped up, grabbed a girl and planted a kiss on her lips.

He'd always watched the proceedings with a bored smile.

When Joe Romano took a woman in his arms, the kiss led to something more intimate than providing a couple of laughs at a stag party.

Except for last night.

Joe slid even further down in the bed, rolled on his belly and closed his eyes. Maybe, if he lay still, his head would stop hurting—and the memory of himself, bending the blonde back over his arm like some second-rate actor in a bad movie—maybe that would go away, too.

It wouldn't. It didn't. How could it?

He hadn't planned it. All he'd had on his mind was how to come up with a polite excuse that would get him out the door before the entertainment started. And then a chunky little man in a chef's outfit had wheeled out a cart topped by the phoniest-looking cake in the world.

"Here comes the babe," the guy next to Joe had murmured happily.

And the next thing he'd known, a blonde in a teeny-weeny bikini had come sailing up out of the top of the cardboard cake as if this were the Olympics and she was determined to take the gold in diving.

Unfortunately, she hadn't.

A hot-looking babe? Definitely. Joe rolled onto his back, put his hands beneath his head and smiled at the ceiling. Gook on her face, but the basics had still been visible. The bottomless green eyes. The elegant, straight nose and the razor-sharp cheekbones. A soft, sexy mouth, so artfully made up that it almost looked as if she wasn't wearing lipstick. No smile on the mouth, but hey, you couldn't expect a babe like that to have everything.

Not even, as it turned out, a way to make a graceful exit from the cake.

To put it bluntly, the lady was a monumental klutz.

While the top part of her had been coming up out of the cake, the bottom had gotten tangled in the cardboard. Or in something. Whatever, Blondie had emerged maybe halfway and then she'd gotten this panicked look, started to flail her arms around...

Which was when he'd gone into his Sir Galahad act, Joe thought, wincing as he rubbed his hands over his stubbled face.

The leap onto the stage. The quick move, grabbing her and hoisting her free of the box.

And then, that kiss.

That kiss. Not just a kiss. A long, deep, hot kiss. And for no good reason, except that she was there and so was he.

Well, yeah. There'd been a reason. It had to do with the stunned look in her eyes, and the soft feel of her in his arms. The smell of her, too. Gardenias, maybe. Or roses. The old-fashioned kind.

"Hello, honey," he remembered saying, and then he'd given her the kind of long, appreciative look her face, her figure, her sexy outfit demanded...

Until he got to her feet, and those shoes. Those homely, sensible, I'm-not-what-you-think-I-am shoes. He'd wanted to laugh. To tell her that a woman with her looks could wear clogs, for all he cared, and she'd still look like—

Like what? a clear, calm voice in his head had said.

Like a woman who needed to be kissed, he'd thought in response.

That was when he'd kissed her.

If only he could stop the action right there. Just stop it, cut it, edit it out like a bad piece of videotape...

Joe sat up. There was no getting away from the memory, the part he'd never live down.

The part when Blondie, without a moment's hesitation, balled up her fist and caught him with a right, just behind his ear.

"Double damn," Joe muttered, and swung his feet to the floor.

The other guys had loved it. The leap. The kiss. Her swing. His yelp of surprise. Her squirming out of his arms and rushing off-stage with the little guy in the white suit running after her...

Oh, yeah. He'd made an ass of himself, all right.

"Bozo and the Bachelor Party," Joe said, and huffed out a breath.

"Way to go, Romano," somebody had yelled.

"Drunk as a skunk, huh, Joe?" some other wag had shouted.

He'd let them think so. It made things easier on the old ego if people thought he'd had one too many, but the truth was, he hadn't. A glass or two of wine at Nonna's and a bottle of beer at the party weren't enough to turn a man's brains to mush.

By the time they'd served what they'd humorously called a midnight supper at the bachelor bash, he was hungry. But, after one cautious, awful bite, he'd put down his fork. Whoever had hired the caterer deserved to be ridden out of town on a rail.

Joe sighed.

After the night he'd had, was it any wonder his head hurt? First that unwanted gift from Nonna. Then a shot to the head from Blondie, although it really hadn't hurt anything but his ego. You'd think she'd been wearing a nun's habit instead of a handful of stretchy stuff sprinkled with glitter...

The phone rang. He grabbed it and growled hello before its vicious trill could puncture his eardrums.

"Joe, my man. How're you doing?"

Moving nothing but his eyes wasn't easy, but Joe managed. According to his alarm clock, it was just after seven.

"You'd better have a good reason for calling me at this hour," Joe said sourly. He winced at his brother's chuckle. "And hold down the noise, okay?"

"I guess that answers my question," Matt said. "Big night, huh?"

"Long night. " Joe winced and snatched the phone from his ear. "What's that noise? Sounds like a semi, blasting an air horn."

"It is," Matt said cheerfully. "Susannah and I are on our way to the airport. We're flying to New York for a long week-end."

"Yeah. Great."

"You could manage to sound a little more enthusiastic."

"That's about all the enthusiasm I can work up in the middle of the night."

"It's not the middle of the night."

"It is, for civilized people."

Matt laughed. "See? I told Susie it wouldn't be a good idea to drop by."

"Damned right. I've killed people for less."

"Yeah, I told her that, too. So we decided we'd phone to wish you a happy birthday in advance."

"A happy…" Joe raked his hand through his hair. "What is this, a family project? First Nonna, now you."

"Nonna told me about the gift she gave you."

Joe heaved a sigh. "She did, huh?"

"She means well," Matthew said, and chuckled.

"It isn't funny."

"At least she seems to have backed away from the Get Joseph Married plan."

"The good news and the bad news," Joe said, and sighed again.

"Well, happy birthday, baby brother."

"Thanks. And remind that gorgeous wife of yours that I'm available any time she's ready to admit she made a mistake."

"Keep dreaming."

Joe laughed. "Have a good time in New York," he said, and hung up the phone.

Okay. He felt a little better now. Still, he moved gingerly as he headed for the bathroom. A pair of aspirin would improve things.

Cautiously, he fingered the skin behind his ear where Blondie had hit him. A grin crept across his mouth.

Who'd have thought such a delicate-looking woman could have clobbered him like that?

Delicate, was right. Almost fragile. There hadn't been much of her, when he'd held her in his arms. Well, that wasn't true. She was small, and slender, but the package was nicely put together.

High, round breasts. A waist his hands could almost span. Good hips. A sweet, firm little butt. And long, long legs. He let his eyelashes droop to his cheeks as he thought about those legs, how it would feel to have them wrapped around him in a moment of blind, blazing passion.…

"Oh, for God's sake, Romano," he muttered.

He stepped into the shower, turned the water on and gasped as the icy spray beat down on his head and shoulders. After a couple of minutes, he adjusted the temperature to something more reasonable.

That was better. Much, much better. So he'd acted like a jerk. Who cared? If there was one thing he'd learned early in life, it was not to look back and regret what you'd already done. A mistake was a mistake. You chalked it up to experience and moved on.

Actually, when he thought about it, he couldn't blame the other guys for laughing. Joe's mouth twitched as he worked shampoo into his hair. He'd have laughed, too, if he'd been the watcher instead of the watched. The kiss hadn't meant a thing, not to him, not to Blondie, despite her protest. Not when you considered her choice of professions.

By the time Joe stepped out of the shower and grabbed for a towel, he was feeling a whole lot more cheerful. Cheerful enough to whistle softly through his teeth…

Right up until the moment the doorbell rang.

His good mood faded. Somebody at the door, now? On a weekend morning? Joe's eyes narrowed. Nobody he knew was foolish enough to risk annihilation by turning up on his doorstep at such an ungodly hour.

Well, one person would. Joe grinned, knotted the towel around his hips and made his way downstairs. The bell rang again, just as he was opening the door.

"Matthew," he said in a prissy, high-pitched voice, "I swear, if you can't bear the idea of going away for a couple of days without first giving me a big, fat, juicy birthday kiss…"

But it wasn't his brother on the porch, it was a woman. A small, slender woman clutching two huge shopping bags and with a suitcase at her feet. Her pale hair was skinned back so tightly it was a wonder her eyes weren't on either side of her head. And those eyes—their color slightly blurred behind smoked, wire-rimmed glasses—those eyes were staring at him as if he were her worst dream come true.

As if he were standing there nearly naked, and waiting for another man's juicy kiss.

Joe could feel heat shooting up into his face.

"Look, miss, this isn't what—I mean, it isn't—I mean, I'm not..." He hissed out a breath. What was he doing, explaining himself to a stranger? Any broad who went door to door at seven something on a Saturday morning had to take what she got, no excuses asked or given.

Funny, though. There was something about her. Something that made him think he'd met her before...

"Mr. Romano?"

Joe nodded. "Yes?"

"Mr. Joseph Romano?"

"That's my name, honey. What do you want?"

Lucinda swallowed hard. Oh, this was fine. Just fine. She'd spent the entire night—well, most of it—pacing the floor of the bedroom she'd once called home, alternately wishing she'd done more than slug last night's idiot and worrying about this morning's interview, until, finally, she'd told herself to forget last night. It was over.

Today—this meeting—was what counted.

Then why was she standing on her new employer's porch with her mouth hanging open and her brain on hold?

Say something, she told herself, something more than his name... But honestly, did he think this was a proper way to come to the door? Naked. Well, almost naked. And—and talking about juicy kisses from a man named Matthew—

"Lady?" Her prospective employer's words dripped with impatience. "If you want something, you'd better spit it out."

Lucinda's eyes narrowed. Men. They were all alike, whether they were pretending to be superstuds like that jerk last night, or like this jerk this morning. One had thought nothing of grabbing her and kissing her, while this one figured it was perfectly fine to answer a door wearing nothing but a towel.

What *did* she want? For him to put on some clothes, for starters. He was so big. So tall. So broad-shouldered, narrow-hipped, and long-legged. That handsome, strong face. The ruffled black hair and sexy blue eyes...

And he liked men, who gave him big, fat birthday kisses.

A good thing, too. No way would she ever share a house with a man who looked like this. No way would she ever share a house with a man—a real man—at all. They were all sneaky, self-serving SOBs. Just look at the way her ex-fiancé had treated her. And that Neanderthal last night…

What had he looked like? Without her glasses, the man had been a blur. A big blur, but a blur, nevertheless. And it had all happened so quickly. Jumping from the cake. Her feet tangling. The man's arms going around her. Hard arms, holding her against a hard body. His husky, teasing voice. That mouth, coming down on hers. Claiming hers. Heating hers…

Joe scowled. He folded his arms over his chest. "Lady, if you have something to say, say it. I haven't got all day."

Lucinda took a fortifying breath and fixed her gaze to his.

"I'm sorry. I, ah, I just wasn't expecting…"

"Before you get yourself in gear, I already gave at the office."

"You what?"

"I said, I've already donated to whatever you're collecting for. Girl Scouts. Boy Scouts. Penguins in Peril. You name it, I gave to it. And if you want a bit of advice, lady—"

"Lucinda. Lucinda Barry. But—"

"…advice you'd do well to heed in the future," he said, his voice rising over hers, "try remembering that the take would be better if you waited until a decent hour to start knocking on doors."

"The take?" Lucinda frowned. "I'm not asking for donations, Mr. Romano."

"Yeah, yeah, that's what they all say. You want to sell me magazines, right?"

"No, sir. As I said, I'm Lucinda Barry, and—"

This time the name registered. Joe blinked. "Bari?" he said, giving it the same rolling "r" as his grandmother.

Lucinda shook her head. "Barry. B-A-R-R-Y."

Joe's eyebrows rose. "Did you say your first name was Lucinda?"

"Yes." Her eyebrows rose, too. "Is that a problem?"

"No. Of course not. It's just that my grandmother told me it was Luciana. I'm surprised she got it wrong."

Lucinda forced a smile to her lips. "It's an easy error to

make, I suppose, for an elderly woman who doesn't speak much English.''

"My grandmother? But she speaks…'' What did it matter? Luciana or Lucinda, the woman was here. Joe cleared his throat. "So. You're the—the cook," he said, staring at her and congratulating himself for not saying what he'd been thinking, which was, "You're the lesbian.''

"I—'' Yes, Lucinda reminded herself, absolutely, she *was* the cook. Didn't the certificate in her pocket prove it? The fact that Chef Florenze hadn't wanted to give it to her was immaterial.

"You have ruined me," he'd screamed after they were back in the kitchen and he'd said she wasn't going to get her certificate, after all. But her fellow students had rallied to her defense, crowding around with grim faces, and finally Florenze had yanked all the certificates from his pocket and thrown them on the floor. "Take them," he'd snarled.

Of course, he hadn't give her the two hundred and fifty dollars. But she had that piece of paper, the one that counted, in her pocket.

"Yes,'' Lucinda said proudly, and straightened her shoulders, "That's who I am, Mr. Romano. I am your birthday gift.''

Joe winced. He looked around to see if any neighbors were out on their own porches and could possibly have overheard what she'd said. This proper-looking martinet with her annoying, unmistakably Bostonian accent, was hardly what a man wanted as a "gift.''

For once, his grandmother hadn't stretched the truth. Lucinda Barry, of the pulled-back hair, the wire-framed glasses and the shapeless skirt and blouse, was truly a dog. A veritable bow-wow.

"Great," he muttered, grasping her arm and hustling her inside the house.

Lucinda held her breath, as if that would keep her body from brushing against his. It was difficult to imagine that body—that very hard-looking, masculine body—as belonging to a man who would, uh, who would accept a juicy kiss from another man.

The shopping bags shifted. She made a wild attempt at recovery but it was too late. The one in her right arm tilted, spilling some of its contents to the floor. She bent down. He did, too.

"I'm sorry," she said quickly. "I'm not usually such a—"

"Klutz?"

Something in the way he said the word made her look up. They were almost nose to nose, and the way he was staring at her made her uneasy.

"Yes. It's just that—" She frowned. A little prickle of awareness danced along the skin at the nape of her neck. "Have we—have we met before, Mr. Romano?"

His eyes narrowed. "I was about to ask you the same thing."

"I don't—I don't think so."

"No." He cleared his throat. "No, I'm sure we haven't."

Of course, they hadn't. A man would remember a sad little mouse like this, if only because she was such a mouse. Joe began collecting the things that had spilled from the bag. A small strainer. A thing with a sharp end that looked like a dental tool gone mad. Another thing that seemed to be a cross between pliers and a—a—

Her smell. Gardenias. Or maybe old-fashioned roses, the kind Nonna grew behind her house...

Again their eyes met. He saw a flush rise in Lucinda Barry's cheeks. Good cheeks. Really good. Sharply defined, elegant, razor-sharp bones...

Joe frowned, got to his feet and held out the thing that looked like pliers.

"What in hell is that?" he said brusquely.

She rose, too, and ran the tip of her tongue across her lips. He fought back the sudden, almost overwhelming need to follow the simple motion of her tongue with his thumb.

Good God, he was losing his mind!

"It's—it's a garlic press."

"A garlic press," he repeated.

"Uh-huh." She reached out for it. Their fingers brushed, and he heard her catch her breath. "You know. For—for pressing garlic."

"For pressing garlic," Joe echoed. What was happening here? For a second, when her hand touched his, he'd felt as if he were having an out-of-body experience, almost as if a bolt of lightning had flamed through his veins. He was pretty sure she'd felt it, too. Looking into her eyes, he'd seen a flash of emerald-green behind the smoky lenses.

A thought flew into his head, then flew out again. A crazy thought, one not worth considering.

"...the kitchen?"

Joe cleared his throat. "Sorry. What did you say?"

"I said, could I see the kitchen, please? That is—that is, if I'm hired."

"Hired?" Joe offered a thin smile. "My grandmother hired you, not me."

"Yes. Of course, Mr. Romano. But there was always the chance you wouldn't—wouldn't want me."

"Why, Miss Barry." Joe's smile tilted. "What man in his right mind wouldn't want you?"

She didn't just blush, she turned crimson. Joe frowned. Why was he teasing her? He was in a foul mood this morning, yes, but it was all because of the woman in the cake. There was no reason to let it out on Lucinda Barry. It wasn't her fault his grandmother had "gifted" him with her presence, any more than it was her fault he'd been a jerk last night.

"There are those who wouldn't," she said politely.

One corner of Joe's mouth curled up in a smile. The woman was hard on the eyes. She didn't like men. But she had starch in her backbone. Good. That way, she wouldn't fall apart when he axed her in a couple of weeks.

"They'd be fools," he said smoothly, "considering how well you cook."

"That's, um, that's very kind, sir. But, ah, but I'm still new to this, and—"

"Not to worry, Miss Barry. My tastes are simple." His smile turned genuine, almost friendly, and he slipped his arm, companionably, around her shoulders. "You won't find me the least bit demanding."

"I'm sure I won't, Mr. Romano." Lucinda stepped away from him and smiled, too, very politely. "Perhaps we can discuss your favorite foods later today, so I'll know which ones please you."

"Well," Joe said, and grinned. "I'm definitely a sap for a Big Mac and fries."

He waited for her to smile but she just went on looking at him as if she was afraid he was suddenly going to toss her over his shoulder and make off with her. Okay, so looping an arm around her had been an error, but he'd meant it as a peace offering. Bad move. Evidently, having a man touch Miss Lucinda Barry was not the way to put her at ease.

"Steaks," he said. "I like steaks, charred on the outside, rare on the inside."

Still nothing. Joe took a deep breath and tried again.

"Of course, I love anything Italian. And my grandmother says Italian dishes are your specialty."

"She did?"

"Nonna was very impressed that you'd studied in Florence."

Florence? As in, Italy? The garlic press slipped from Lucinda's hand. It looked as if Joseph Romano's grandmother had gotten more than her name wrong, but Lucinda had the feeling this wasn't the time to tell him that, or to point out that the only time she'd visited Florence had been in her senior year at Stafford, when all the girls, her included, had gathered around the statue of David and gaped at his, um, his masculinity.

"Uh, yes. Well, actually, I do lots of different sorts of things. French. Spanish. American." She cleared her throat and bent down to retrieve the press. "You know how it is."

He didn't, but he wasn't about to ask. Joe had bent down for the press, too. Now, he was staring at his new cook's feet. They were small feet. Delicate, probably...despite the fact that they were shod in very sensible shoes.

Sensible. Not white, but sensible.

Joe stood up, so quickly that he almost bumped heads with his new cook, and shunted the insane thought out of his head.

"That garlic press seems determined to get away," he said with a strained smile. "I— I, ah, I take it those shopping bags are filled with other tools of your trade?"

"Tools of my... Oh. Yes. Yes, they are."

"And, ah, your luggage...?"

"It's on the porch."

"Right. Well, then, why don't we stow these bags in the kitchen first, and I'll bring in the rest of your stuff."

"You don't have to do that, Mr. Romano. I can manage."

She reached for the bag Joe was holding. He pulled it back. She tugged at it again and all but dragged it out of his hands.

"Really, Mr. Romano. I can manage. You just go ahead and put some clothes on..."

Her voice trailed away. Oh, God. Had she really said that? She must have, based on the look on her new boss's face. But it was all his fault. So what if he liked men? He still made her feel uncomfortable, standing around half naked, putting his arm around her shoulders...

And then there was that nagging feeling she'd met him before.

"I—I didn't mean," she began, and Joe laughed.

"Yes, Miss Barry. You *did* mean. And I apologize. I'd forgotten that I was walking around in a towel."

"Yes, sir. But— Really. I'm sorry, sir. I only meant—"

"Look, Miss Barry. We're going to be living together for a while. Sharing the house, I mean. Why don't we try a little less formality, okay? My name is Joe. And yours is... Lucy?"

"It's Lucinda."

It figured. Joe shifted the bag and stuck out his hand. She looked at it as if she'd never seen a man's hand before. Slowly, carefully, as if she were reaching for a hot iron instead of his fingers, she took it.

Bzzz. There it was again. That kick, as if he'd put his finger in a lamp socket.

She snatched her hand back.

"One of us isn't grounded," Joe said with a little smile.

"I guess not," she said, and flicked her tongue across her bottom lip.

Another kick, this time just from watching that pink tongue. Joe smothered a groan along with the thought that maybe he really was losing his mind.

"Well," he said briskly, "I'll go get dressed. You take a look at the kitchen. And then we'll get your luggage and I'll show you to your rooms."

"Fine." She waited, smiled pleasantly, then cocked her head. "Where is it? The kitchen, I mean?"

"Ah." Joe nodded. "Just down the hall, to your right."

"Thank you, Mr. Romano."

"Joe," Joe said, and smiled.

"Joe. Well, then. I'll just put these things away…"

She flashed him a polite smile. He smiled back. Her sensible heels whispered against the tile floor as she hurried down the hall.

Joe watched her go. The bags she held bulged in all directions. He could hear the faint clink of glass and metal with each step she took. She had to have enough gadgets and gizmos with her to open a small…

His eyes narrowed.

She was wearing a skirt and blouse, and those sensible shoes. All in all, she looked about as stylish as his sixth-grade teacher. Still, there was something unusual about her.

Each time she put one foot ahead of the other, her hips swayed, ever so slightly, beneath that skirt.

He stared, transfixed. Left, right. Left, right. It was ladylike. Ladylike in extremis, he thought with a little smile. But the view was pleasant. She had a nice walk. A nice pair of hips. Small, but nice. A nice bottom, too, and he had to admit, he was a man who admired bottoms. She had good legs, too. Long. At least, he figured them for long. It was hard to tell, because the skirt dipped below her knees.

Were her legs as long as Blondie's? Were they as silken and elegant? It was a stupid thought, but harmless, wasn't it? To wonder how his new lady chef would look dressed in Blondie's spangles and thong…

Joe blinked.

What was the matter with him this morning? His new chef was a bow-wow from any angle but this one. She was also a woman who liked other women and, old-fashioned as it might be, if there was one thing he couldn't understand, it was that scene.

Left, right. Swing, sway…

Joe frowned.

Time for another shower, he thought, and headed back up the stairs at a trot.

CHAPTER FOUR

LUCINDA stood in the center of Joe Romano's kitchen, blew a strand of hair back from her forehead, and wondered how she could have gotten herself into such a mess.

She was in trouble.

Real trouble. Up-the-river-without-a-paddle trouble. Every-cliché-she-could-think-of trouble, and there was no way out.

She didn't like Joseph Romano or his kitchen. And yet, dammit, she was stuck with both of them.

Well, no. Carefully, Lucinda placed the shopping bags on top of a granite counter. She had nothing against the kitchen. Who would? The refrigerator was big enough to house a family of polar bears. The pot rack bristled with what looked like a fortune in copper and stainless steel. You could have roasted a moose in the double wall ovens, if moose was to your taste.

Who could dislike such largesse, especially if that person were a cook?

And that, Lucinda admitted with a sigh, that, was the problem. She wasn't a cook, despite the certificate that marked her as a graduate of the San Francisco School of Culinary Arts. She was an imposter, trained by a pompous little man who—why not admit it?—owned a bogus school. She'd sensed it, almost from the beginning, but the price of the course had been more than a match for her level of desperation.

Half a dozen bentwood stools fronted a long length of granite counter. Lucinda pulled one out, eased up onto it, put her elbows on the counter and rubbed her hands over her face.

She was trapped. Trapped in an advertisement from *Better Homes and Gardens,* with a man she'd disliked on sight.

Joe Romano's grandmother had lovingly described him as her darling, but grandma's "darling" was an arrogant, self-centered, gorgeous hunk of masculinity. Well, maybe that was

48

the wrong word to use, Lucinda thought uneasily, although he certainly struck her as masculine.

Whatever. That was his business. Her business involved cooking for him.

Lucinda groaned, folded her arms and laid her head down.

Who was she kidding? She couldn't cook, not really, and Romano would figure that out for himself soon enough. How she'd thought she'd get away with this charade was beyond her.

No. No, it wasn't. She sat up straight and stroked back the strands of hair that had pulled loose from the knot at the nape of her neck.

She'd thought she could do it because cooking for a gay man would ease her into things. Gay guys were easygoing. They were non-threatening. They weren't demanding.

Joe Romano didn't fit the bill.

For all his smiles, she sensed he was about as easygoing, as nonthreatening, as undemanding as a stick of dynamite.

What would it be like, to work for him if he were straight?

"Are you crazy, Lucinda?" she said, and sat up.

Who cared? The man's sexual preferences were of no interest to her. Let him do what he wanted, with whom he wanted. What if he *had* been straight? Women made so much fuss about sex and, really, what was the point? The whole thing was overrated. She'd always known it, in her heart, even before her mother had dropped those not terribly discreet hints about What Men Wanted From Women.

Sex, was what they wanted. It was the nature of the beast. Men needed sex, like the boor last night. He might even have seen himself as some sort of Don Juan.

Well, she'd shown him how she felt about that.

Her arm still ached from the blow, but it had been worth it to see the way the bastard's head snapped back, the way he'd looked at her, as if he couldn't imagine a woman rebuffing his advances.

Some probably wouldn't.

Her vision might have been blurry but all her other senses worked just fine. When he'd caught her in his arms, she'd felt the heat of his body. The power of all those very masculine muscles. The hardness of his mouth, and then the softening of it as he fitted his lips to hers. The feel of his hand, threading into her hair...

Lucinda shot to her feet and began unloading kitchen equipment from the bags.

That was one thing to be said about Joseph Romano's sexual preferences. He wouldn't have hot-and-cold running females going in and out the door at all hours.

No. He'd have hot-and-cold running males instead.

The thought wasn't comforting.

"Oh, hell," she said weakly, and pulled open a drawer.

Light from the overhead spotlights glinted on a breathtaking array of stainless steel tools. She picked up one and turned it over and over between her fingers.

What was it? She had no idea. Actually, she had no idea what this whole room was about. You'd need a doctoral degree in physics to operate the stove; you'd have to be fluent in Cuisinart to turn on half the appliances lined up along the counters—

"Finding everything all right?"

Lucinda spun around. Joseph Romano was standing in the doorway. Actually, he was lounging in it, arms folded, his body leaning back against the frame. He was fully dressed, for which she was eternally grateful. Dressed as a man like him would, of course, not properly as in the circle in which she'd grown up, but dressed, nevertheless—if you could call a white T-shirt that clung to all those muscles "dressed." If you could call those jeans "dressed." They were faded. And snug. Oh, so snug...

She blinked.

"Just fine and dandy," she said, shooting him a bright smile and shutting the drawer with her hip. She swung away from those piercing blue eyes and went back to unloading the shopping bags, laying things out on the counter as if her life depended on it.

"Fascinating."

Lucinda jumped again. He'd come up behind her. She could feel the faint warmth of his breath on her neck.

Goose bumps rose on her skin.

"Do you really need all those gadgets to cook a meal?"

"Oh, not all of them." She flashed another smile as she slipped past him. "Actually, I don't know that I'll need my things at all. You have a wonderfully equipped kitchen."

"Well, if kitchens could talk, mine would probably be shouting hosannas." Joe slid a hip onto the edge of a stool and smiled. "In gratitude at your arrival, that is. I'm not much of a cook."

An understatement. Maybe even a flat-out lie, but the lady would never know it if he kept as far out of her realm as he could manage and let her take over in here, not just for a couple of weeks but indefinitely.

The more he'd thought about it, as he'd showered and dressed, the more he'd started to think that this might just work out. Maybe his nonna hadn't been so wrong. A woman who could cook up a storm, with a desirability quotient of zero, living right under his roof and available day or night to whip up a meal or a snack, was starting to sound like a pretty good asset. Better than good, he thought as his stomach rumbled a reminder that he'd yet to have breakfast.

So, he'd be a little nicer. A bit more friendly. It wasn't his cook's fault she wasn't a looker any more than it was her fault she didn't like men.

"I know."

Joe jerked his head up. Lucinda had wandered away again. She'd opened a drawer and she was looking down into it, her brows drawn together as if she'd found something either unmentionable or unnamable inside.

"Sorry?"

"I said, your grandmother mentioned you didn't do much cooking." Why had she picked this drawer to open? There were beaters in it, for a mixer. She recognized those, but not those other things, the long, wicked-looking hunks of shiny, twisted metal. What on earth could they be?

"What are those things, anyway?"

This time she managed not to jump when she heard Joe Romano's voice behind her. When she felt his breath on her neck. Was he going to keep doing that? Sneaking up when she didn't expect it? Hadn't the man ever heard of the importance of personal space? She didn't like the intrusion on hers. It was too close. Too intimate.

Her pulse rate skidded uneasily.

"What things?" she said, and slammed the drawer shut.

Joe reached past her and yanked it open. His shoulder brushed hers; his scent, a combination of soap and man, rose to her nostrils. He was doing it again. Surrounding her, as that—that miserable creature at the bachelor party had done last night.

Lucinda sniffed, then sniffed again. His smell was so clean. So masculine.

So familiar.

"Lucinda?"

She blinked. "Yes, Mr. Romano?"

"Joe," he said, and smiled politely.

"Joe," she repeated, and cleared her throat. "I'm sorry. Did you say something?"

He lifted one of the twisted spikes of gleaming metal from the drawer. "I was wondering what these are."

"Uh, ah, those?"

"Yeah. When I first bought this house, I was, uh, I was going with this wo—with this person who figured to get me interested in something long-term by showing me the joys of domesticity." *Have to watch that, Romano. You date babes, but so does she.* Somehow, the thought was distressing. "Toni's house-warming gift was to have the kitchen completely equipped with every conceivable gadget."

"Ah. Well, Tony did a great job."

"Yeah, but the first time I went looking for a teaspoon, I pulled open this drawer and saw these things. And I've been trying to figure out what they are, ever since."

Lucinda nodded. "Well, ask Tony."

"Oh, Toni's long gone," Joe said lazily. He looked at his

new cook. "Do you always wear your sunglasses in the house?"

"My…? Oh. No. These aren't sunglasses. They're smoked, that's all. Actually, I usually wear contacts. But I lost one yesterday and when I found it this morning, I didn't have time to clean it properly, so…"

Joe nodded, as if he were listening, but he wasn't. Actually, for such a drab little mouse, she had an interesting mouth. Soft. Full. Nice hair, too. A strand had escaped and hung against her temple. Incongruously, it reminded him of the long, sexy hair of the babe who'd popped out of the cake. Could Lucinda's hair possibly feel as silken? His fingers itched with the desire to find out. Maybe even to taste that mouth…

Hot damn.

"So," he said briskly as he took a couple of quick steps back, "what do you do with these spiked things, anyway?"

Lucinda smiled brightly. "Why don't you try and guess?"

"I did try. I decided they must be a medieval torture device." He chuckled, leaned against the counter, crossed his feet at the ankles and tossed the metal object from hand to hand. "But the guy I bought the place from wasn't into S and M."

"S and…" Lucinda swallowed. This was more about Joe Romano's sexual preferences than she wanted to know. "I see. But, uh, I mean, there's nothing wrong with S and M. If you're into it. Not you. Someone else. Well, two someone else's. If two people are adults, if that's what turns them on…"

Her eyes met Joe's. Color flooded her face. "It's a dough hook," she said, the name for the spike coming back to her in a rush. She plucked it from his hand, dumped it alongside its mate, and slammed the drawer shut. "A person's private life is his private life, is my motto, Mr. Romano. I hope you understand that."

She saw color flood his face, too. "Of course," he said stiffly. "That goes without saying. I'd never sit in judgment on anyone, Lucy."

"Lucinda," she said primly. "And, if you don't mind, I'd like to see my accommodations."

"Certainly. If you'll follow me…?"

She nodded and fell in behind him. Backs rigid, they marched through the house and up the stairs.

Lucinda sat on the edge of her bed, hands folded neatly in her lap.

She'd put her clothing away, lined up her shoes in the closet, hung her robe on the hook in her private bathroom and put her toothbrush into the holder on the sink.

"I hope your accommodations are to your liking," her new employer had said.

She'd assured him that they were fine—even though they weren't.

Chef Florenze had discussed accommodations. He'd talked about living in the staff quarters of hotels, small inns, and private homes.

"For those of you fortunate enough to find positions as personal cooks to the wealthy," he'd said with a supercilious little smile.

Not that she'd needed the information. She knew how things were done in the home she'd grown up in and in those of her childhood friends. Family lived on one floor, staff on another. A cook might sleep on the staff floor, or in rooms just off the kitchen.

Whatever the arrangement, it didn't include putting a cook into the bedroom next door to her employer's, with the headboards of their respective beds separated by a thin wall.

It didn't matter, she thought briskly. So what if Mr. Romano slept a foot away from where she slept? So what if they might bump into each other in the hall? She would block her mind to the pictures racing through it.

Pictures that would be even worse if he were straight and she had to imagine him in that room, in that bed, with a woman...

Lucinda frowned. "Ridiculous," she said, and got to her feet.

It was time to brave the dangers of the kitchen, check the fridge and think about making dinner tonight.

"Are you going out?" she'd asked Mr. Romano after he'd shown her to her rooms.

He'd seemed to hesitate and then he'd shrugged and said yes. Yes, he was.

"And will you be here for dinner?"

He'd hesitated again. "Yeah," he'd finally replied, "yeah, I will."

So she had almost an entire day to work up a menu. Good. That gave her plenty of time to figure out how to prepare a meal he'd never forget.

Lucinda hesitated at the door. Should she change into her uniform? She was unclear as to the protocol. Chefs wore white in restaurant kitchens but in private homes, in her experience, anyway, such things were generally left to the discretion of the employer.

What would Mr. Romano prefer?

Lucinda bit her lip. She had to stop thinking of him that way. Informality. That was the thing to remember. He'd made that very clear and the last thing she wanted to do was to get on his wrong side because, despite his attempts at small pleasantries, she was fairly certain that was where she almost was.

But for what reason?

Perhaps he resented his grandmother's interference. Perhaps he didn't like the idea of having a woman in his life. Well, not in his life. In his home. After all, he was—he was—

He was gorgeous, was what he was. So big. Such wonderfully broad shoulders. So much muscle. And that face. The dazzling, sky-blue eyes. The lean cheeks and tough-looking jaw. The sexy stubble on it.

Lucinda shut her eyes and wondered if the idiot last night had looked anything like that. No, of course not. He couldn't have looked anything like her boss. Not too many men did.

Not too many kissed like the one last night, either.

It was all still so vivid. The husky voice whispering, "Hello, honey." The hard mouth, the softening of it against hers as what had begun as a teasing kiss suddenly turned hot and dangerous...

Surely, not many men kissed that well.

That well?

Lucinda rushed to the closet and grabbed her white jacket and white trousers. Quickly, she stripped off her clothing, put on her chef's outfit and sensible white working shoes.

She was a chef. A professional person. Perhaps looking like one would make her think like one again.

The house was quiet. Empty, she knew, save for her. Knowing that, she searched for a radio when she reached the kitchen, found it housed in what looked like an oversize sugar cube and switched from station to station until she found something worth listening to. An aria from *La Bohème* filled the room with glorious sound.

Now, what could she make to impress her employer? The better question was, what could she make that would be edible? She hadn't emptied everything out of her shopping bags, not with Mr. Romano standing by. She had a couple of cookbooks stashed away. A fat volume titled *Haute Cuisine*. Another called *Mangia Italian*. And, just in case, a slim one titled *Even You Can Learn to Cook*.

Between them, she'd surely come up with—

"Hot damn," a male voice said, "who's dying?"

Lucinda shrieked and spun around. Joe Romano glared at her from the doorway.

"Dammit," she said, "you're going to have to stop doing…" She caught herself, sank her teeth lightly into her bottom lip, and blushed. "Mr. Romano. Joe. Forgive me. It's just that I—I thought you were out."

"Obviously." He strode across the room and turned off the radio. "The thing does that, goes on all by itself sometimes. Sorry. I should have warned you."

Lucinda drew herself up. "It did not go on by itself. I turned it on. I'm sorry if my taste in music annoys you."

"That was music? That woman screaming at the top of her lungs?"

"It was opera," she said stiffly. *"La Bohème."*

"Well, there's no accounting for tastes, I guess."

"No," she said, even more stiffly, "there isn't."

He smiled. It was a devastating smile. She wondered if it meant anything to him that he had a smile women all around the world would gladly die for.

"Ever try listening to some sixties' rock-and-roll?"

"No."

The smile became a grin. "Well, that's plain enough. No 'maybe.' No 'I don't think so.' Just a simple, unadorned 'no.'"

"I'll be sure not to play my music when you're home, sir."

"Oh, lighten up, Lucy."

"Lucinda."

"Whichever. You can play your music anytime you like. Just keep it down to a roar, okay?"

She nodded. "Certainly, sir."

"Joe. And I didn't mean to startle you."

"You have every right to startle me. I mean, you have every right to be in your own kitchen. It's just that you said you were going out."

"I did. I went for a run."

"And came back and showered again," she babbled before she could stop herself. Color swept into her face. "I, uh, I can tell. I noticed. You changed your shirt. And your jeans. You shaved, too. There's no stubble on your jaw. And your hair is—it's wet..."

Her boss was staring at her as if she'd lost her mind, and maybe she had.

"Well," she said brightly, "I'll see you tonight, Mr.—Joe." She flashed what she hoped was a smile. "About what time do you prefer dinner?"

"Seven, seven-thirty is fine." Joe sauntered across the room and eased onto a stool. "Actually, I haven't had breakfast yet. And I thought—"

"You thought?" Lucinda said politely, and then she blinked. "Oh. Would you like me to make you something?"

"If you wouldn't mind."

"Mind? No. No, of course not."

She felt her heart give an unsteady thump as she turned away, but how difficult could breakfast be? She knew how to scramble eggs. She could even make waffles, so long as she checked with the cookbook. Pancakes, too, unless her luck ran out and they stuck to the griddle.

"Let's see," she said, almost falling into the stadium-size fridge as she peered inside. "What do we have? Ah. Eggs. And bacon. And seven-grain bread." She turned and smiled at him. "Bacon and eggs, and toast. How does that... Is something wrong?"

Joe was staring at the floor. Or at her feet. Had she stepped in something unmentionable? No, she thought, looking down. No, her white shoes were as pristine as half an hour's worth of polishing each night could make them.

"Your shoes." Slowly he raised his eyes to her face.

"Yes?"

"They're, um, they're very sensible."

Those were his words, but his eyes said something else. The blue had gone the color of a midnight sky, and a pair of vertical lines had appeared just between his black eyebrows.

"I know," Lucinda said, trying not to sound as puzzled as she felt. "I'm on my feet a lot. And kitchen floors are usually hard. Wood, or tile..." Her voice trailed away. He was looking at her feet again, as if he'd never seen feet before. Or as if he had, but never feet quite like hers. First opera, now sensible shoes. Life was not going to be easy in this house. "Is there a problem with my shoes, Mr. Romano?"

His head came up. His eyes were still dark, still impossible to read.

"No, of course not." He smiled, though she thought it looked as if it hurt his lips to do it. "Well. You were saying you'd make bacon and eggs, is that right?"

"Yes. If that's okay with you."

"Sure. Bacon and eggs would be great."

Joe watched as his pale blond, flower-scented, sensibly shod, high-cheekboned, soft-mouthed little cook opened one cabinet drawer after another, searching, he figured, for a skillet. He began to rise, to help her find one, then thought better of it. Her cheekbones. Her smell. Her hair. Her mouth, and now her shoes...

Okay, two and two didn't necessarily add up to four. Learning that had helped him make his first million. Still, the best thing to do, when in doubt, was to sit back and observe. That was another principle he'd picked up on his way to the top.

Lucinda. Little Lucy, he thought, narrowing his eyes, I am just going to sit here and watch.

After a lot of clattering, she found what she'd been looking for. She took a big pan from a cabinet and put it on the stove. Then she opened the package of bacon and slipped out several strips.

Even Joe knew that laying the stuff in a skillet, without turning on the heat beneath it, was not going to work.

"You have to turn the burner on," he said.

"Oh, I know that." She kept her back to him but he could see the stiffness in her shoulders. "It's just that I've never seen a stove quite like this one."

Well, that was possible. The stove was a high-tech monster. Nobody had ever seen anything like it, except Toni, who'd oohed and aahed as if it were the Hope diamond. If his new cook wasn't mechanically inclined, she could, indeed, have trouble figuring out how to operate the thing...

On the other hand, the dials that said On and Off were pretty easy to distinguish.

"You have to push that button on the back. That's it. Now touch the pad to the right. There you go."

"Thank you."

"You're welcome." He waited a minute, watched as she took out the eggs, found a bowl, and broke them into it, trying not to wince when most of one egg plopped onto the counter. "Tricky little devils," he said pleasantly.

"Mmm," she said, breaking another one.

A chunk of shell fell into the bowl. Delicately, she fished it out.

Joe folded his arms. "How about some coffee?"

"Coffee?"

"Yes. You know, that black, caffeinated stuff that kick-starts the day."

"Coffee," she repeated, and shot a sideways look at the two

coffeemakers lined up on the counter. One was a drip filter. The other was a spaceship. "Is—is drip okay?"

"I thought cappuccino would be nice."

"Cappuccino."

"Yes."

"Cappuccino," she said again, but very softly. His eyes narrowed as she touched the espresso machine with one finger, then reached for the steam spigot.

"On the other hand," he said quickly, "why don't we stay with drip?"

Her sigh of relief was audible. "Where do you keep the coffee?"

"In the freezer. The grinder is right there, near the—"

"The coffeepot. Yes, I saw it."

There was a funny tightness to Joe's voice. Lucinda stole a glance at him as she took the beans from the freezer. There was a tightness to his mouth, too. And his eyes had gone from midnight-blue to black.

A shudder rippled down her spine. Resolutely, she ground the beans—she always ground her own, so that was a snap. Then she put up the coffee and swung towards Joe.

"Well," she said, her voice resonating with false good cheer, "how would you like your eggs? Scrambled?"

"Fried."

There was a certain quality to his tone, a smugness. Did he think she couldn't fry a couple of eggs? Frying was even easier than scrambling. Well, of course, it was a good thing he hadn't asked her to fry them, then turn them so that the yolks cooked gently without breaking. Over-easy, was the restaurant parlance, though she couldn't imagine why. Flipping eggs without smashing the yolks wasn't easy. It was impossible. For her, anyway. She'd never mastered the—

"Fried," he said softly, "and over-easy. I like the yolks done but not runny, Lucy."

"Lucinda." The correction was automatic. The quaver in her voice was not. "Certainly, sir."

"Joe." His smile was sharp and quick. "If there's anything I hate, it's to have my yolks broken."

If there's anything *I* hate, she thought savagely, it's dealing with a smug, smarmy male.

"No problem, Mr. Romano." She waited for him to tell her, again, that his name was Joe. He didn't. "I never break the yolks."

It was a lie. She always broke them, but she would not break them this time. Until now, she thought she'd passed the interview with Joseph Romano but, quite clearly, this—this ridiculous Flipping Of The Eggs was the true test.

Her new boss was sneaky.

"I tell you what, Lucy."

"Luc—"

"I'll make the toast. How's that?"

"Oh, it's not necessary…"

"Sure it is."

His arm brushed hers as he made his way to the bread drawer. So did his shoulder, and his hip. How come he had to pass so close to her in this enormous kitchen?

"If I do the toast," he said, "you'll have all the time in the world to concentrate on the eggs."

Lucinda nodded. The eggs.

She took out another skillet, put in a lump of butter, waited for the butter to melt. She remembered, too late, that she should have heated the pan first. Instead, centuries ground past as she—she and Mr. Romano—waited for the butter to melt.

"You can—you can sit down, sir," she said.

Joe's smile glittered. "Thank you," he replied as he leaned back against the counter, "but I'd rather stand and watch you. It's fascinating, watching a pro at work. Which reminds me…" He nodded towards the pan. "The butter's turning brown."

Oh, God, it was. Lucinda grabbed the bowl that held the eggs and dumped it over the skillet.

"I prefer letting the butter brown. It gives the eggs a piquant flavor."

"Mmm. Cooks them awfully fast, too. Just look at that."

She looked. The eggs were crisping at the edges.

"Just about ready to flip, wouldn't you say?"

She flashed Joe a look. "Yes. Yes, they are."

His eyes bored into hers. "Flip them, then," he said, and what she heard in those words turned her blood to ice.

Lucinda took a deep breath, reached for a spatula and held it poised over the eggs. Please, she thought, please, please, please...

The yolks broke. The whites fell apart, those that hadn't already toasted to inedibility. She stared into the pan, at the gold-and-white mess, and tried to will the yolks to roundness, the whites to wholeness.

"My," Joe purred, "that didn't work out too well, did it?"

Lucinda shot him a cold look. He'd been hoping she'd fail, she just knew it.

"No," she snapped, "it didn't." Several locks of hair fell into her eyes. She blew them back, blew them back again, then thrust her hand through the hair in a useless attempt to shove it behind her ear.

"Probably just as well the bacon's burning." Again, he gave her that all-teeth smile. "I mean, what's the point of bacon without eggs?"

"The bacon...?" Oh, it was. The skillet was sending up clouds of dark smoke. Lucinda leaned towards it. Grease splattered against her eyeglasses. She grabbed them, tried to pull them off but one earpiece caught in her hair. She swore, tugged the glasses free, and her hair tumbled over her shoulders as she reached for the pan.

"You little fool!" Strong hands caught her by the shoulders and pushed her aside. Joe grabbed a dish towel, grabbed the skillet and dumped its smoking, sizzling contents into the sink. Then he swung towards Lucinda.

The look on his face made her heart rise into her throat.

"You're no more a cook than I am," he growled.

"You're right. I mean, you're wrong." She lifted her hands, as if in supplication. "I mean, what I am is—"

"I know just what you are, *honey*."

The word, and the way he said it, echoed and re-echoed through the room. Lucinda put her hand to her throat.

"No," she whispered. "No. It can't be. You can't be—"

Joe's mouth twisted. "On the contrary, *honey*. It is. I am. And if you need proof…"

Before she could say a word, he pulled her into his arms and kissed her.

CHAPTER FIVE

HE HADN'T planned on kissing her.

Why would he kiss a lying, cheating blonde with few scruples and no morals?

Especially if she was a...

Forget that.

Anyway, he knew why he was kissing her. What better way to prove that he knew who she was and what she was?

The scam was over. Last night, Blondie had worn a handful of spangles instead of this silly white suit. And he'd been the guy who kissed her.

Now he was kissing her to make sure she knew it.

She was struggling against him, trying to twist her face away from his, but he wasn't finished with her. He was making a point and after he'd made it, he'd let her go. Until then, he'd keep her right here, in his arms.

Right here, her soft body against his.

Her breasts against his chest.

Her mouth, promising a sweetness unlike anything he'd ever tasted before...

With an angry cry, she wrenched her mouth from his.

"You bastard! Let go of me!"

He would. He knew that. He'd never believed any of that bull about a woman of her sexual orientation changing her mind in the arms of the right man.

He'd let her go. Any minute now. Any second.

Joe groaned, thrust his hands into Lucinda's silky hair, lifted her face to his and kissed her again.

"You," she hissed against his mouth, "you..."

"That's right, honey," he murmured. "Me."

Her eyes burned with rage but even as he looked deep into

the cool, green depths, he saw the anger change to something else, something that made his blood run thick.

"I said, let go of me."

But she whispered it this time. And her hands lifted, closed over his wrists and clasped them.

"Let go."

Her voice shook, and her lashes fell to her cheeks. Her lips parted and Joe drew her even closer, bent to her again and kissed her. Her mouth was warm and pliant. She moaned; he thought he did, too.

"Lucy," he whispered, and then her hands were in his hair, she was lifting herself to him, his tongue was deep in her mouth and he was tasting her.

Sweet. So sweet. The taste of her was like the smell of her, a mix of gardenias, wild roses and violets.

He wanted more.

He shifted his weight, drew her closer so that she was leaning into him, the contours of her body melding with the length of his. He felt the fullness of her breasts, the soft pressure of her thighs, the heat of her, all around him.

She was trembling. Trembling in his arms like a leaf in a gentle breeze. And she was whimpering, making the sounds a woman makes when a man is loving her, sounds that were going to drive him crazy if he didn't have her soon.

Joe leaned back against the wall. He slipped one arm around her hips, lifted her, cupped her bottom and brought her against him. He was as hard as a rock, harder than a man could possibly be, and he moved against her, wanting her to know, to feel what she'd done to him.

What only she could undo.

"Oh," she whispered, "oh..."

Her head fell back as he took his mouth from hers and pressed it to her throat. He licked her soft skin, sank his teeth gently into her flesh. She tasted like honey, felt like silk.

He was drowning in all of it, her taste, her smell, the pliant feel of her heated body in his arms.

Now. That was all he could think. He was beyond anything else, beyond talking or hearing. All that mattered was his need to possess her. Her need, to be possessed. She was clinging to him, sobbing his name, giving back kiss for kiss.

Her zipper hissed as he opened it.

"No," she said, but he knew the word had no meaning because even as she said it, she was helping him free her of those silly white trousers.

He lifted her to the countertop. She was so beautiful. Her eyes were dark with desire, her mouth pink and swollen from his kisses. Her hair tumbled around her face like molten gold.

Joe's hands shook as he stripped his T-shirt over his head and undid the top fastener on his jeans. He wanted to strip off her jacket, see her breasts. Touch them, and taste them. And he would, the next time, but now the need to have her was too close to insanity.

His control was fast slipping away.

He ran his hands lightly over her thighs as he moved between them. She felt like satin, even to his callused fingertips.

"You're beautiful," he said softly.

Lucy moaned as he stroked the narrow band of cotton that shielded the center of her femininity from him. He put his hand over her, cupped her, and she arched back, her body taut as a drawn bow.

A cry broke from her throat.

"Now," he said hoarsely. "Now."

Yes. Oh, yes. That was what she wanted. To give herself to him, now. To have him take her, now. To be his—to be his—

His what?

Lucinda's eyes flew open. The room whirled around her, straightened, and she saw everything, the dark-eyed stranger standing between her legs, the man who'd humiliated her last night and was doing it again, this time, with her help.

She was revolted by it. His actions. Her response. Revolted, and horrified. She came off the counter in a blur.

"You," she shrieked, "you—you—you…"

Those weren't the cries of a woman in ecstasy. Even Joe, stumbling backwards, still caught in a haze of sexual heat as he tried to fend off her blows, figured that out.

"You no-good, rotten, evil, cold-blooded son of a bitch..."

She tried to claw at his face. Joe grabbed her wrists and forced her hands to her sides.

"Not cold-blooded," he said. "Those other things, maybe, but definitely not—"

"It *was* you!" Her eyes were a wild, vivid green. "You were the one who pawed me last night!"

"Pawed you? Baby, I saved your pretty little ass. If I hadn't grabbed you, you'd have made an entrance nobody in that room would ever forget."

"You—you kissed me, you bastard!"

Joe folded his arms over his chest. "Which kiss are we talking about, Lucy?" He narrowed his eyes and flashed a quick, humorless smile. "The one last night, when you tried to deck me?"

"I wish I had, you rat. And it's not Lucy, it's Lucinda. How many times must I tell you that?"

"Or the kiss just now. The one that ended up with you trying to climb me like a cat shinnying up a tree."

She snarled, showed her teeth, charged him. Joe laughed, grabbed her by the arms and shoved her back against the counter.

"I should have known," Lucinda panted. "I should have known it was you!"

"Yeah, well, you would have, if you'd been wearing your glasses." He smiled coldly. "Glasses spoil the image, I guess, is that right, baby?"

"Unhand me, Mr. Romano."

Unhand me, Mr. Romano? Joe laughed again. She was really something, this babe. A second ago her choice of language had suited the kind of woman she really was. Now she was doing her best to sound like a heroine straight out of a Victorian novel, but heroines in Victorian novels didn't pop out of cakes wearing teeny-weeny bikinis.

She might be able to fool some people, but not him.

Not after the last few mind-blowing minutes.

Lucinda Barry was one clever broad, but he wasn't the village idiot. He knew what she was, a woman who lived by her wits. She could fool a guileless old lady. She could make a man think she was Scheherazade and he was the sultan.

She was a woman who had a kiss that was a weapon. A kiss that could turn a guy into a quivering mass of jelly. Hormonal jelly. Which, he thought coldly, was the only kind of jelly his gorgeous, conniving, let's-pretend cook would know anything about.

The more he found out about her, the more questions he had. Why would a woman so beautiful make herself up to look like the head of the Spinsters Forever Foundation? Why would a woman who made her living turning men on, be into what San Franciscans politely called an alternative life-style?

Why would she want a job as a cook?

A cook.

Joe blew out a noisy breath. Lying Lucy was as much a cook as he was. That she'd managed to make a pot of coffee without a recipe was just short of a miracle. Which brought him back to the beginning. Who was she? Why had she taken this job? And what did she want of him?

"Who are you?" Joe demanded gruffly.

"You know who I am. I'm Lucinda Barry."

"Come on, lady. You know what I mean. What do you want here?"

Lucinda twisted against the grip of his hands. "You're hurting me."

"Tough." He knew he was; he could feel his fingers pressing on the fragile bones of her wrist, but her bones were the only things fragile about Miss Lucinda Barry—if that really was her name. "I asked you a question, honey, and I want an answer."

"Don't call me that."

"Honey?"

He laughed. Lucinda could have killed him for doing it. This was the second, no, the third time he'd laughed since he'd grabbed her and all but forced himself on her, and it made her hate him even more.

How could such a thing have happened?

She'd been so excited about this job. About working for a

sweet-tempered, easygoing man. Instead she'd found herself employed by an arrogant exhibitionist who ran around in a smile and a towel and behaved as if he owned the world. Now, to find out that this—this boor was the person who'd dragged her out of that cake, who'd made her look even more ridiculous than she felt...

She hadn't wanted to believe it, not even after he'd called her "honey" in that horrible way that made the word sound obscene, or after he'd pulled off her glasses and she'd stared at him long enough to let the blur of the prior night and the reality of her black-haired, blue-eyed, wide-shouldered employer merge into one hateful image.

She'd had no choice but to believe it once he kissed her.

There was no mistaking the kiss, or those strong arms. The powerful body. The hard mouth—a mouth that had somehow tricked hers into softening beneath it, into making her blood thicken until her heart almost went into overdrive.

A shudder of rage raced through her body.

The bastard! Thinking he could treat her like some—some little slut. Thinking he could kiss her and get away with it.

Thinking he could behave as if he liked women. As if he wanted a woman. Wanted her.

Outrage gave her the strength she needed. With a wrench, she pulled one hand free of his, knotted it into a fist and pounded it against his chest.

"I am not your honey," she said furiously. "In fact, just hearing the word come out of your mouth makes me sick."

"You're breaking my heart," Joe said as he captured her hand and stilled it. "And you still haven't answered my question. Who are you?"

"You know who I am."

"What I know is that the Mary Poppins get-up is phony."

"Mary Poppins was a nanny. I'm a cook."

"Lucretia Borgia was a better cook than you."

Lucinda stiffened. "I am a graduate of—"

"Yeah." Joe grinned, a feral show of gleaming white teeth. "I can just imagine what you're a graduate of. The last I heard, they don't teach broads to cook in those places."

"Your mind is even more filthy than your insinuations! And your grandmother told me you were a gentleman!"

"I am, when I'm dealing with a lady. Once again, gorgeous. What are you doing in my home?"

Gorgeous? Her? Was that what he thought? She wasn't "gorgeous," she never had been. She was well-bred. Well-mannered. She could use a fish knife. She knew the difference between tea and high tea.

But "gorgeous"? Her? Did he really think…

Oh, God. She was standing here, arguing with a half-dressed ape who evidently batted from both sides of the plate, wondering if he really thought she was gorgeous—and she didn't have her pants on.

Where were they? On the floor? On the counter?

On the toaster, where Joe Romano, the most evil of evil men, had flung them.

Lucinda drew herself up. "Let go of my wrist."

"I will, after you answer some questions."

"I am not answering anything until I put on my pants."

Joe blinked. Her face had turned bright red but she was holding her ground. And she was right. She was still standing in front of him dressed in a white chef's jacket, white panties, white shoes…and nothing else.

And no wonder. Her pants were draped over the toaster, like the debris that remains after a hurricane passes.

He smiled, snagged the pants. When she grabbed for them, he lifted them just out of her reach.

"These, you mean?"

Lucinda folded her arms. "Just give them to me."

"Sure." Joe twirled the pants on one finger. "As soon as you tell me what I want to know."

Her face turned even redder. "Give me those pants," she said, and lunged. It was definitely a bad move, because it brought her right up against Joe Romano's hard, naked chest.

Her heart gave a quick, stumbling beat. She pulled back, put as much space between herself and him as she could manage, and glared.

"Stealing a woman's clothes, Romano? Is that the only way a man like you can get a woman naked?"

It sounded like a good line to her, but Joe only grinned. "Anybody who knows me can tell you how wrong you are, honey. Now, let's come at this like reasonable adults. You want the pants? I want answers. Sounds like a fair trade to me."

Lucinda blew her hair out of her eyes. "All right," she said grimly. "What do you want to know?"

"That's my girl."

"I am not your girl. I am not your anything, except your cook."

"I know. And I appreciate it, Lucy, I really do. Why, the finest restaurants in town were begging you to take over their kitchens, and instead you opted to work for me." Joe slapped the hand holding the pants over his heart. "The thought brings tears to my eyes."

"Your questions, Romano. And then, my trousers."

Joe's smile faded. "Question one. What are you doing in my life?"

"You know the answer to that. I'm your birthday...." Lucinda frowned. "I'm your cook. I'm here at your grandmother's request."

"And where, pray tell, did my grandmother find you?" His slow, knowing smile sent a shiver up her spine. "Under a cabbage leaf in her garden?"

"She answered an ad I ran in the paper."

"An ad in the paper."

"Yes, that's right. You know, the paper. Newspaper. Some people read them. Some even manage to do it without moving their lips."

"Somehow or other, I don't think my nonna spends much time reading ads like the one you must have run."

Lucinda flushed. "'Wanted,'" she said stiffly, "'position as live-in cook in a small household. References upon request.'"

"Ah," Joe said softly. "And you supplied those references?"

"Your grandmother interviewed me. She hired me on the spot and said references weren't necessary."

Joe's mouth twisted. "How fortunate for you, hmm?"

"I have references," she replied even more stiffly. "You're welcome to check them."

"Lots of satisfied customers, huh?"

Don't rise to the bait, she warned herself. That was what he wanted, to get her riled enough to lose her temper.

"This is my first job as a cook. I told that to your grandmother."

"And she said?"

"She said it would be the perfect first job for me, that you were easygoing and sensitive."

Joe's brows lifted. "Sensitive?"

"She also said even the most basic meals would be an improvement over the junk she suspected you ate." Lucinda smiled thinly. "You grandmother foolishly thought it important to provide you with nutrition. I, on the other hand, prefer to think that you manage to take your sustenance from chunks of old cheese without springing the trap."

"Oh, that's funny. Very funny. Do you do that as part of your act? I bet it wows them."

"My act?"

"Sure. You know. A little bump, a little grind, toss out a clever line as you toss off the G-string."

"The only G-string I'm familiar with is the one on a violin," she said, though she had a good enough idea of what he meant to make her blush. "And I want my trousers."

Joe looked at her, taking his time, his eyes going slowly from her feet to her face.

"Seems a pity," he said softly, "to cover up so much of your talent."

"Dammit, Romano, you gave me your word!"

"And you haven't fulfilled the terms of the deal. What's the real reason you took this job?"

"I needed it," she said bluntly. "I had to find a place to live in a hurry, I'm almost flat broke because I spent every penny I had on the course at the culinary institute, and I'd made up my mind I'd sooner scrub bathrooms than flip one more greasy hamburger. Any more questions?''

Joe cocked his head as he looked at her. She sounded serious enough, but somehow he couldn't imagine her scrubbing bathrooms. Not when she could look like this. Not when she kissed and sighed so that a man was tempted to believe it wasn't all an act, that she really wanted him.

"It's a great story. But for a babe who claims to know all about flipping hamburgers, you don't seem very at home in a kitchen," he said, and tossed the pants to her.

She stepped into them so quickly she stumbled, and her hand went out automatically to steady herself. Her fingers brushed his chest. A surge of unadulterated lust shot through his loins and he gritted his teeth against the crazy desire to sweep her into his arms, carry her to his room and finish what they'd both started.

"Your kitchen," she said loftily, "is not the usual sort of kitchen."

Joe took a slow look around him. "Stove, sink, fridge. Nothing unusual, as far as I can see."

"It's very high-tech."

"High-tech, as in you couldn't figure out how to turn on the stove?"

"I admit, I'm still—I'm still perfecting my art." She felt her face redden when he barked out a laugh. "I'm happy to provide you with such hilarity, Mr. Romano."

"Sorry. It's just, well, it's surprising to hear a woman who carbonized the bacon and massacred the eggs refer to her talents as 'art.'''

Lucinda lifted her chin. "I'm learning," she said quietly. "I'm not ashamed to admit it."

Joe looked down into her flushed face. Her eyes glittered, but with what? Anger? Hurt? Perhaps, even, pride? Dammit, he couldn't figure her out.

Last night she'd looked like an example of every man's dream, except for the silly white shoes. Moments ago, in his arms, she'd been that dream come true—until she'd slugged him and cursed him.

And yet he had the feeling she could hold her own at a formal dinner in the White House.

Not that it mattered.

The woman was no more a cook than he was. Somehow she'd wormed her way into his grandmother's good graces and into his life, but no way was she staying there.

"Look," he said as politely as he could, "this has gotten out of hand. I mean, you're not, uh, not comfortable with my kitchen. Besides, I don't need a cook. So—"

"You do. And I need this job." Her voice quavered. He looked at her in surprise, saw a lifted chin, a determined jaw— and desperation in her green eyes. "I admit, your kitchen took me by surprise. If your grandmother hadn't told me you didn't know the first thing about cooking..." Her words trailed away.

"I don't follow you."

"Well..." She sank her teeth lightly into her bottom lip. He watched the simple action, felt his belly knot, and told himself to stop being an idiot. "Well, because she said that, I didn't expect you to have all this fancy equipment. I mean, normally, the high-tech stuff wouldn't surprise me, in the home of a man of—of your persuasion."

"A man of...?"

"Yes." She lifted her eyes to his, blushed, and looked away. "See, if she hadn't told me that—"

"That I can't cook," Joe said like a man carefully repeating words spoken in a foreign tongue in hopes of figuring out what they meant.

"Right." Lucinda smiled slightly. "But, of course, if you *could* cook, she wouldn't have hired me."

Joe cleared his throat. "Is all this leading somewhere, Miss Barry? Because right now, I'm pretty well lost."

She took a deep breath, exhaled it slowly through her nose.

"What I'm trying to say is that we had a big book about appliances at the institute. It covered everything from simple gas ranges to convection ovens to glass cooktops, and if I'd stopped to think, I'd have checked through it."

"Because?" he said, still in that baffled tone.

"Because," Lucinda said patiently, "even though you can't

cook, I suppose it stands to reason you'd have an elaborate kitchen. I mean, everyone knows that men like you love to putter in the—'' She caught the look on his face and stopped. This probably wasn't the time to talk about his condition, but it was too late to go back, and she knew it. ''Everyone knows that,'' she said briskly, ''and I should have figured that even if *you* didn't like fussing around in here, your, uh, your—''

''My?'' Joe said helpfully.

''Your, uh, your male friends might.''

Joe thought about the guys he supposed she'd call his ''friends.'' Jack could whip up a mean taco salad, but that was about it. All of them ''cooked'' the same way he did, via take-out.

''That's a fascinating explanation, Lucy.''

''Lucinda,'' she said automatically. ''Thank you, Mr. Romano.''

''Joe. Frankly, though, I don't know what the hell you're talking about.''

''Yes, you do. Men of your persuasion—''

''Dammit, that's the second time you said that. Men of *what* persuasion? Venture capitalists? Soccer players? Guys with blue eyes?'' His patience snapped. Joe reached out, caught hold of Lucinda's elbows and lifted her to her toes. ''What are you babbling about?''

''And that's heaven only knows how many times you've been vile!'' Lucinda grunted as she twisted, uselessly, against that powerful grasp. ''I should have figured a couple of minutes of sane, decent human behavior were all you could manage, and never mind what your poor, downtrodden grandmother said about your sweet temperament.''

''You leave her out of this! My grandmother isn't poor or downtrodden.''

''She must be,'' Lucinda said furiously, ''otherwise, you'd never be able to get her to say you were good-natured.''

''I am good-natured,'' Joe shouted, while the veins stood out in his neck. ''And sweet-tempered. And whatever else Nonna told you. I am all of those things. I always have been. I was born that way.''

"There's no need to try and convince me. Plenty of people are already debating the topic."

Joe's head shot forward. "People are debating my disposition?"

"Oh, for goodness' sake! You know what I'm talking about." Angrily she shook herself loose of him, or he let go of her, whichever. Either way, it was a relief not to have his fingers pressing into her flesh. How could a man who wasn't really a man be so strong? How could he have kissed her and turned her into melting butter? "One thing's for sure, Romano. You most definitely were not born with a pleasant temperament."

"I was, too," Joe said, and hated himself for sounding like a six-year-old.

"You weren't." She stepped back, massaging her elbows and glowering. "I not only believed your grandmother, I bought into the stereotype that all gay men are sweet and kind. Even the ones who don't like to cook!"

"That's crap! Being gay has nothing to with…"

Being gay?

Joe could feel the blood draining from his head. Gay? Was that what she'd said? "Gay?" he wheezed. His mouth twisted; he told himself to be calm. He'd misunderstood her, that was all. "You don't think I'm…you can't possibly believe I'm…"

One look at his paper-white face and Lucinda wished she could call the words back. She had the feeling that the trouble she'd found herself in just a few hours ago was nothing compared to this. Maybe he wasn't "out." Maybe he wasn't happy having people know the truth about him.

How come she hadn't thought of that?

"Look, Mr. Romano." Her voice was hoarse with nerves and she cleared her throat. "Honestly, it's none of my affair what your personal preferences are. If you're still in the closet, you can count on me to keep—"

"I'm not in any damned closet."

His voice was a low growl. The color was returning to his face but too rapidly, as if the blood were erupting from an underground geyser.

"My nonna couldn't have said— She couldn't think—"

"I'll keep your secret, if that's what's—"

"Hot damn!" Joe spun away and dug his hands into his hair. Then he swung back towards Lucinda, his eyes wild. "Does she really think that's the reason I haven't married? Because I'm—I'm—"

"Gay?"

"I'm not. Dammitall, woman! Not that there's anything wrong with it, but I'm not!"

Lucinda stiffened. "You don't have to take that tone with me. You may be an arrogant, mean-tempered, unpleasant, hateful, no-good rat, but I told you, your personal life is your affair."

"You're damned right it is," Joe shouted. He clenched his jaw, shut his eyes and counted silently to ten before he looked at her again. "Look," he said very calmly, "I don't know where my grandmother got this idea, but I assure you, I am a perfectly normal man. I like women. I *love* women. I don't want to boast, but half the good-looking females in this town can vouch for my—my virility."

"Whatever you say, Mr. Romano."

Joe did another mental ten-count, went to twenty, and wondered what the penalty could be for murdering your own grandmother.

You can vouch for it, he almost said to Lucy, but what would that get him? He was a regular guy but she—hell, he'd done his best to forget what she was, although how a woman could come to life in a man's arms when her tastes ran to—ran to...

He really didn't want to think about that.

Joe grabbed his shirt from the floor and tugged it down over his head.

"Look, lady. I'm straight. I always have been, and I have to admit, I don't understand anybody who's into something different. It's not natural. It's not normal. The male of the species, the female of the species..." Whoa. He was getting lost here. He took a breath. "What I'm trying to tell you is that I think any other arrangement is crazy. Not that I'm condemning you for your preference, of course."

Lucinda blinked. "I beg your pardon?"

"I'm heterosexual," he said, jabbing his thumb into his chest. "But what you are is your own concern."

"Huh?"

"It's what you are, and that's all there is to it."

"I'm a cook, is what I are. Am."

Joe's mouth took on a cynical twist. "Sure."

"I don't like the way you say that," she said coldly. "I *am* a cook, no matter what you think." Lucinda put her fists on her hips. "In fact, it will give me great pleasure to wave my graduation certificate under your nose as I go out the door because, just between you and me, Romano, you know what you can do with this job."

She turned and began marching from the room. Joe strode after her.

"That's fine," he yelled as she made her way up the stairs, "because I don't want a woman like you around. You're either the world's clumsiest stripper or its most lethal cook. And forget what I said about it being okay for you to be what you want to be. Truth is, I know it's not politically correct to condemn anybody for anything in today's crazy world but frankly, *Miss* Barry, I think that babes who are into other babes are—"

"What?" Lucinda spun towards him, her face white. "What did you say?"

"You heard me. Go on, get the P.C. police, for all I give a damn." Joe looked away in disgust and started towards the kitchen. "Nonna," he muttered, "Nonna, you just wait until— Oof!"

Lucinda's balled-up fist got him right between the shoulders. Joe swung around, grabbed her, and shook her, hard.

"Listen," he growled, "I'm tired unto death of…" The rush of angry words stopped. He looked at her, really looked at her, this woman his grandmother had wished on him. He looked at her shocked expression. At her emerald eyes, her soft mouth. He thought of the feel of that mouth under his. Of her sighs and moans. Of the heat he'd discovered when he'd touched her…

And he knew. She wasn't gay, any more than he was.

"You aren't," he said softly, "are you?"

Lucinda knew it wasn't really a question. She shook her head.

"No." She looked up into those dark blue eyes and felt a little breathless. "And you aren't, either."

Joe's smile was lazy and wicked. He dipped his head and kissed her. It was a long, slow, deep kiss and when, at last, he took his mouth from hers, both of them were breathing hard.

"Any questions?"

Lucinda touched her finger to her lips. "Just one." She cleared her throat. "How could you have thought I was—that I was...?"

Joe's easy smile vanished. "The same way you did," he said grimly. "Because of my dear, sweet, innocent, meddling grandmother."

CHAPTER SIX

LUCINDA wasted a few seconds trying to find her voice.

"I beg your pardon?"

"You heard me. My grandmother made up a story, spoon-fed it to each of us, and sat back to see what would happen."

"No. I don't believe it. I *can't* believe it! That sweet, charming little old lady..."

"That sweet, charming, little old conniver, you mean."

"But why? Why would she do this?" Lucinda took a deep breath and told herself to stay calm. "She seemed so—so sane."

"She *is* sane. Her mind would put Machiavelli's to shame."

"Well, maybe she's becoming senile. I had a great-aunt once, my great-aunt Harriet, and she—"

Joe threw up his arms. "I don't give a damn about your great-aunt Harriet," he snarled. "We're talking about my nonna. And trust me, she's not senile. She's not crazy." His jaw tightened. "She's a meddlesome old witch, is what she is."

"Meddlesome?"

"That's right, honey. You want me to spell the word? Meddlesome. M-e-d-d—"

"You know, Mr. Romano, if you'd stop being such a smart-ass..." Lucinda blinked. Where had that come from? "Smart-ass" was not a word in her vocabulary but then, neither were some of the other things she'd called this grim-faced, tight-jawed male pacing around the room. No question about it. The man brought out the worst in her.

Joe stopped and swung towards her. "Oh, don't stop now." He smiled coldly. "You were saying that I'm a smart-ass."

"I was simply pointing out that we might be able to figure

out how this happened, and what to do about it, if you'd stop being so sarcastic."

His smile tilted, grew even more frigid. "There's nothing to figure out, Nonna's done this kind of thing before. Well, not with as much style, but this isn't the first time she's tried to play matchmaker."

Lucinda stared at him. "Matchmaker? You mean—you mean, that's what she was doing? She thought that you—that you and I—"

"Preposterous, isn't it?"

Joe jammed his hands into his pockets, kicked a chair out of the way and resumed his march around the kitchen. His aim was off; his foot hadn't hit the chair squarely and now his big toe stung—but that was okay. Considering the enormity of his irritation, a little pain for somebody, even himself, seemed good.

"It's more than that." Lucinda made a sound that might have been a laugh. "It's impossible. You and I...?"

"You already said that."

She had, hadn't she? But the very idea that anyone would think she could ever, in a million years, be attracted to a man like this, was—it was...

"It's crazy."

"It's vintage Nonna."

"Does she do this kind of thing often?"

"Try and set me up with women?" Joe nodded. "Often enough. And it's never worked. I guess she decided a direct approach wasn't going to do the job."

Lucinda shook her head, sat on one of the stools and rubbed her hands over her face.

"I really don't understand any of this. If she was trying to get us interested in each other, why would she tell me that you were... You know. And why would she tell you that I was—"

"Yeah." Joe kicked the same chair again as he stalked past it. His aim wasn't any better this time, either, and the pain went straight from his toe to the top of his head. Fine. Maybe it would cancel out the headache that had already begun drumming in his temples. "The only thing I can come up with is that she figured she could sneak a live-in lady right through my front door, if I thought that lady wasn't interested in men.''

"No! I mean, that sweet little old woman wouldn't... Your own grandmother wouldn't..."

"Don't look so shocked, honey. A live-in lady as in, 'My, but it's nice to have a female around the house.' As in, 'Isn't it great to find home-cooked meals on the table?''' He looked at her, his eyes as dark as the sea at night. "As in, 'Joseph, if you won't find a good Italian girl on your own, one who can cook all your favorite dishes, I'll find one for you.'''

Lucinda ran the tip of her tongue over bone-dry lips.

"But," she choked out, "but, I'm not."

"You're damned right, you're not." Joe stopped pacing, slapped a hand on the counter on either side of her, and gave her a smile that made her breath catch. "The last word a man would ever use to describe you is 'good.'''

Rising to the bait wouldn't get her anywhere, Lucinda reminded herself, especially when Joe was so close to her that she could almost feel the heat radiating from his body.

"I meant," she said with dignity, "that I am not Italian."

"Your name is. She thought so, anyway."

"And I'm, um, I'm not particularly expert at cooking Italian dishes."

He laughed, but not pleasantly. "You're not particularly expert at cooking anything that requires a pot."

"For your information," she said coldly, "I have some excellent desserts in my repertoire."

"*Gelato,*" Joe said. "That's what snared my grandmother."

"I was not trying to 'snare' her. And are we going to critique my talent in the kitchen, or figure out why she would do such a thing to us?"

"I just explained it to you. My nonna did what she thought would get you into my house." His smile was sexy and dangerous. "As for your talent...aside from that ice cream—and, for all I know, you bought that in North Beach—aside from that, the only place you have 'talent' is in a bedroom."

"Mr. Romano." Lucinda kicked back her stool and got to her feet. Big mistake. He didn't budge, not by an inch, which meant there wasn't more than a breath of space separating them. "Mr. Romano," she repeated crisply, "insulting me won't get us anywhere."

"You keep using that word."

"What word?"

"'Us.' As if there were an 'us.'" He lifted one hand from the counter and stroked her cheek. "Of course, we could change that. For an afternoon, anyway. Hell, you *are* my birthday present."

He'd meant it as a kind of bitter joke, but the feel of her skin under his hand made his breath quicken. He remembered how she'd looked, her eyes wide and blind with desire. How she'd tasted, and smelled.

Unplanned, his fingers slid into her hair and he bent to her and kissed her. He kissed her hard and fast, offering no soft pleasantries or gentleness, and she reacted by making a startled sound. Her hands rose. She pushed against his chest—pushed, until her fingers curled into his T-shirt and her lips parted beneath his...

And then she twisted her head away and jerked back.

"Stop it," she said. Her voice trembled, but then, his kiss had made her knees wobble, which only proved that he was clever, this Joseph Romano, and that she despised him. "I was supposed to be your cook. Nothing else."

"That's your story," Joe said. "You might as well stick with it."

His jaw knotted and he took a step back. That damned smell, the scent of flowers, drifted to his nostrils. How could a broad like this smell so old-fashioned?

"Meaning?"

"Meaning, I'm having trouble imagining my grandmother coming up with this neat little scheme all by herself."

"Well, who could possibly have helped..." Lucinda bristled. "Are you suggesting that I had something to do with this?"

Joe shrugged. "All I know is, she wants me married." His eyes narrowed, became obsidian slits. "And, most conveniently, here you are."

"What nonsense!" Her chin lifted in a gesture of contemptuous defiance. "If I were ever foolish enough to marry, it would never, ever, not in a million lifetimes, be to a man like you."

"Oh, baby, what a disappointment." Each of his words was encapsulated in icy sarcasm. "And here I'd hoped you wanted to be Mrs. Joseph Romano. I mean, what more could a guy want? You're a liar. A scam artist. A woman who can't decide between a career as a stripper or as Lucretia Borgia." Joe's smile glittered with malice. "In other words, the perfect wife."

"The perfect wife for you," Lucinda snapped, "is a blob of plastic lying in a box in an adults-only toy shop, waiting for the moment somebody decides to take her out and blow her up."

"That's witty, Miss Barry. Incredibly witty."

"I thought so."

Her smile was smug and infuriating. Just for a second, he thought about kissing that smile away, about swinging her into his arms, carrying up to his bedroom and unwrapping his gift—but he wasn't that much of a fool.

Besides, he had too many questions. Was his nonna really capable of cooking up such a risky plan? And, if she was, why lie about him to the woman she'd chosen to be his wife?

He couldn't think of a reason. Not one. And that left him wondering, again, if the sexy blonde who could make herself look like a candidate for a convent, who called herself a cook but didn't know how to fry an egg, was somehow involved in the scheme.

Maybe Nonna had only wanted to give him a cook, not a wife. And maybe she'd said that, just that, to Lucinda.

I'd love to give my grandson a cook for his birthday, his nonna might have said, *but I know my Joey. He wouldn't want a woman underfoot.*

And Blondie could have replied, *Why don't you tell me about your grandson, Mrs. Romano?*

And his nonna, who didn't think he knew how much she boasted about him, would have done just that, listed all his manly virtues, including the fact that he was rich and that he wasn't married.

And then Blondie could have batted her lashes and said, *Well, you know, if you really want to convince him that I'm not going to be any sort of problem, you could let him think...*

No. That didn't make sense. Even if that was the way it had gone down, why would Lucinda have thought he was...what she'd thought he was?

Nonna was at the bottom of it, he was certain—as certain as he could be of anything, without confronting her. And when he did, he wanted Lucinda right beside him.

Joe folded his arms and jerked his head towards the door.

"Five minutes," he growled.

"Five minutes for what?"

"To get dressed." His eyes raked her from head to toe. "I'm going to see my grandmother, and you're going with me."

"You're damned right, I'm going with you! I want to know what's going on here."

"Yeah, well, that makes two of us. Change out of that silly suit and let's get going."

"It's not a silly suit, it's a professional uniform. And if you weren't so damned self-centered, you'd realize that I'm the one who's really paying the price for your grandmother's meddling."

"Watch what you say about her."

Lucinda blinked. "But you just said—"

"I know what I said. She's my grandmother, not yours."

Lucinda thought of her stiff-necked, starchy grandmother, who insisted on being addressed as Grandmother Barry and wouldn't have known a hug from a handshake.

"She is, indeed," she said coolly. "And that makes it doubly wrong that she told you an untruth about me."

"Which 'untruth' were you thinking of?" Joe replied even more coolly. "That you could cook? That you're from Italy?" His eyes narrowed. "Or that you're not into men?"

"She misinterpreted everything."

"With a little help from you, maybe?"

"That's not true."

"Yeah, well, let's just find out, shall we?" Joe jerked his head towards the door. "You want to change your clothes, go and do it." He looked at his watch, then at her. "You've already used up three minutes."

"Oh, yes, sir. Certainly, sir. Your wish is my com—"

Lucinda gasped as Joe caught her and pulled her to him. "I'm not in the best of moods, Ms. Barry." His voice was soft, his eyes dangerous. "If I were you, I'd keep that thought firmly in mind."

A tremor ran through her at the brush of his body against hers. For one wild moment she imagined what would happen if she put her hands in his hair and dragged his mouth down to hers.

The thought gave her the strength she needed to pull out of his grasp.

"You're a horrible man!"

Joe grinned. "Sticks and stones, Blondie. They don't mean a thing."

"No?" Lucinda was almost sputtering with rage. "Well, then, try this. As soon as we get back from your precious nonna's, I'm packing my things and quitting!"

"No, honey, you're not."

"Of course I am. If you think I'd stay on in this house with you—"

"You can't quit. You've already been fired."

"Been what?"

"Fired. You know, as in 'terminated.' As in, 'most definitely unemployed.'"

"You're worse than horrible," she said, her voice trembling.

Joe laughed. She fought back the urge to slug him again. Instead, she rushed from the kitchen and hurried up the stairs with the sound of his laughter following after her.

Quitting was one thing, but fired? Fired, by the most arrogant, super-macho stud that had ever walked the planet? He was still laughing, as if what had happened were amusing instead of awful. He was, in fact, guffawing. She could hear him, all the way up here.

"Chauvinistic rat," she muttered, and slammed the bedroom door after her.

Lucinda took off her sensible shoes and put them, neatly, beside the bed. She took off her chef's whites, folded them and laid them over the back of a chair.

"Fired," she said. "That hideous man fired me!"

She stood in the center of the room, heart racing. Then she whirled around, snatched up the white jacket and tried to rip it in half. Panting, she threw it into a corner, flung the pants after it, and kicked the shoes, those damned sensible shoes, against the wall.

"Fired," she whispered, and sank down on the edge of the bed. What now? She had an empty bank account and nowhere to go...

Bang!

Lucinda leaped to her feet and spun towards the door. It shuddered under the pound of Romano's fist.

"One more minute," he yelled, "or I come in and get you."

He would, too. What an awful man Joe Romano was! To think she'd tolerated his kisses...

Tolerated? She'd climbed all over him, just as he'd said. Oh, the embarrassment of it! But it was his fault. The man was a practiced seducer. He'd taken advantage of her at a weak moment...

"Thirty seconds!"

Lucinda pulled on a blouse and skirt, hissing when the zipper jammed. Romano pounded again, just as she stuffed her feet into a pair of loafers.

"Dammit!" She wrenched the door open and glared. "There's no need to break down the door. Of course, I shouldn't expect you to know that. You aren't civilized and you're certainly not the gentleman your poor, deluded grandmother thinks you to be. You probably knock down doors for a hobby."

Joe glared right back. His tight-lipped, tight-mannered, lying, cheating excuse-for-a-cook was a mess. Hanks of blond hair hung in her face. Her blouse was buttoned wrong and hung two inches shorter on the right side than the left. A piece of the tail was stuck in the teeth of the zipper.

She'd probably never looked so disheveled in her life—except, of course, when she was wearing nothing but sequins and a smile and popping out of cakes.

"I, on the other hand," she continued coldly, "am a person of dignity and delicacy. And it's a good thing for you, Mr. Romano, that our relationship has ended, or I would tell you precisely what I think of you, your temper, and your unruly disposition."

It was quite a speech, delivered in rounded tones that spoke of good schools and good breeding. Joe figured he'd probably have fallen for the act, if he hadn't known what Blondie really was.

But he did know, and that changed everything.

"Are you finished making speeches?" he said politely.

"It was a comment, not a speech, but yes, I'm finished, for the moment."

"Actually, you're finished for..." Joe glanced at his watch. "For twenty moments." He looked at her, his face expressionless. "Or thirty. It all depends on traffic."

"I beg your pardon?"

"It's simple. I don't want to hear another word out of you until we get to my grandmother's. Got that?"

Color arched swept along her cheekbones. Those high, elegant cheekbones...

Stop it, Joe told himself tightly, and set off down the stairs.

She ignored what he'd said.

He'd suspected she would. Joe doubted if Miss Lucinda Barry had ever done what she'd been told to do in her entire life. So it was no surprise when, halfway to Nonna's, she gave him a look he figured was supposed to turn him to stone.

"Must you drive this thing so fast?"

"It isn't a thing, it's a Ferrari. And no, I don't have to drive it this fast. I could drive it a hell of a lot faster, if there weren't so much damned traffic."

"There's no need to prove your masculinity to me," she

said coldly. "If you say you aren't—what your grandmother said you were—then you aren't."

"Is that what you think I'm doing?" Joe barked out a laugh. "Talk about being egocentric... I don't want to shock you, Blondie, but I drive fast all the time. I like to drive fast. I love to drive fast. You got that?"

"Certainly," she said in a smug little voice that made him want to pull over to the curb and haul her into his arms again.

Stupid thought, Romano, Joe told himself coldly, and made no response at all.

Ahead, the light went from amber to red. He cursed under his breath, brought the car to a squealing halt and sat tapping his fingers on the steering wheel.

"And," she said, "my name is not Blondie."

"Excuse me?"

"You keep calling me that, and it isn't my name."

Joe's jaw tightened. "Anything else?"

"Only that you needn't take out your anger on me. I'm the innocent party in this sordid affair."

He shot her a sideways look. "Are you, now?"

"What's that supposed to mean? A little old lady planned this. Do I look like a little old lady to you?"

What she looked like was a disaster. Her hair was still a mess, her buttons were still closed wrong, but she'd crossed her legs and her skirt had risen up and up, until it lay high above her knee, exposing a length of slender, tanned thigh. She probably knew it, too. The prim and proper act was just that. It was as phony as a three dollar bill, and only a fool would respond to it.

But oh, that was an interesting bit of skin. He knew what it felt like, too. Silky. Warm. No, not warm. Hot...

The light changed. He jammed his foot down on the gas pedal and the car shot away hard enough to leave rubber behind.

"I know what you're thinking, Romano."

Joe looked at her. "You only wish," he said coldly.

"Wish what?"

"That I'm thinking what you think I'm thinking. What you

hope I'm thinking." Hell, he sounded daft. A muscle knotted in his cheek. "You're wasting your charms on me," he growled. "You might as well get that through your head."

Lucinda frowned. "I don't know what you're talking about."

"The hell you don't."

"If what you're thinking is that I had something to do with this charade, you're wrong."

"I am, huh?"

"Yes, you are."

Lucinda recrossed her legs. The sound of nylon whispering against nylon made the hair rise on the back of Joe's neck.

"I know exactly what happened," she said, "Things are starting to make sense."

"Sense," he said, and forced himself to concentrate on the road. "Sense, how?"

"Your grandmother was confused."

Joe gave a short, unpleasant laugh. "And you had nothing to do with that, right?"

"As much as you choose not to believe it, that's correct. She wanted a live-in cook. I wanted a job, and I needed a place to live. The situation seemed ideal."

"Oh, yeah." Joe's words were rimmed in icy sarcasm. "I'll just bet it did."

"Mrs. Romano phoned me," Lucinda said primly. "And we set up an appointment."

"And when you got to her place, she told you she had a grandson who needed a cook."

"Exactly."

"Or maybe," he said, his tone hardening, "maybe what she told you was that she had this rich, single grandson, and you thought, 'Bingo!'"

"What I thought," Lucinda said, ignoring the remark, "and what I said, was that if he were single and lived alone, I couldn't possibly accept the position."

Joe braked for another light. "Why not?"

"Because."

"Oh, that's an excellent answer, Blondie. So definitive. So informative. So full of—"

"Because," she said sharply, "it would be improper."

"Improper" wasn't even on the list of possible answers that had flipped through Joe's head.

"Improper?"

"Exactly."

He looked over at her again. She was staring straight ahead, her face flushed, her hands knotted in her lap.

"Improper, because I wouldn't be comfortable living in the same house with someone of the opposite sex. I told that to your grandmother. It wasn't easy because—well, you know this, of course—her English isn't very good."

Joe flashed Lucinda a sharp look.

"It isn't, huh?"

"No. Surely, you know that."

The light changed. Joe gunned the engine, shifted gears, roared up the street and made a hard right into his grandmother's driveway. What he knew, he thought grimly, was that it must have been an irresistible combination. A scheming old lady and a scheming young one. It was a match made in heaven...

Or in hell.

He shut off the engine. In the sudden silence he could almost hear the sound the hammer would have made as the nails sealed his coffin.

"Your grandmother finally seemed to understand my concerns," Lucinda said.

Joe swung towards her. She sounded as prim and proper as she had when he'd opened the door to her that morning. She almost looked it, too.

But she wasn't prim or proper. Not if she entertained at stag parties. Not if she went up like dry tinder at the touch of a match, in a man's arms.

"And then she made it clear that propriety wouldn't be a problem because her grandson was—"

"Gay."

"Exactly."

Joe grunted. "And you saw that as a challenge."

"No. Of course not."

"What, then? As a reclamation project? As a guy you could turn into the kind of male who'd be butter in your hands?"

"Are you crazy? What I saw was that I'd be safe." She looked at him. "If you were gay, I wouldn't have to worry about you making unseemly advances."

Unseemly advances, he thought coldly. This, from a woman who'd been sitting on his kitchen counter an hour ago, her thighs open to his touch.

"And then she asked me if I liked men. Well, I told her I didn't, not since my fiancé had... What's the matter?"

Joe sprang from the car, pulled open her door, grabbed her hand and tugged her onto the sidewalk.

"Nothing," he said as he hustled her up the steps to the front door. "Everything! Hell, what a setup. I'm just wondering what jury in the world would possibly convict me for non-nacide after they heard this whole—"

The door swung open. Nonna Romano stood in the entry, a smile as innocent as sainthood on her face.

"*Giuseppe,*" she said, and opened her arms in welcome. "And Luciana. Come in, come in."

"It's Lucinda," Joe said grimly. He maneuvered past his grandmother, his hand still wrapped around Lucinda's wrist. "And you can cut the '*Giuseppe*' stuff. We're going to conduct this little talk in plain old American."

His grandmother swallowed nervously. Her black eyes darted from Lucinda to Joe and back again.

"Something is wrong? I look out, I see your car, I see that you do not come around to the back door the way you always do, *Gius*—Joseph."

"You bet there's something wrong," Joe snapped. "Did you tell this—this person...that I was..." He took a deep breath. "That I didn't like women?"

Nonna's eyes darted from face to face again. "No. Yes. I mean, women like her. Forgive me, *signorina,* but I knew you were not my Joseph's type."

"Her English is much better than when I met with her," Lucinda hissed. "I can hardly believe it's the same woman."

Joe smiled tightly. "Oh, it's the same woman. Isn't that right, Nonna?"

Nonna stepped back. "Joseph," she said in a soft, sweet voice, "*mio bambino,* I just put a tray of manicotti in the—"

"Never mind the manicotti." Joe let go of Lucinda's elbow and folded his arms. "You told her I didn't like women. And when she told you she'd just broken off with a boyfriend—"

"A fiancé," Lucinda said. "Back home, in Boston. I told her that, and I said I was really off men, that I'd never want to get involved with one again."

"Is that what she said, Nonna?"

"Well—well, maybe. It's so long ago. You know how things are, Joey, when a woman gets old and feeble..."

"It was a week ago. And you're about as feeble as Godzilla."

"Joey. I meant well."

"You always mean well," Joe said sternly. "But this time, you've gone too far." He put his arm around Lucinda's rigid shoulders and dragged her forward. "Do you know what you've done, Nonna?"

"Yes," Nonna said with a wide-eyed smile. "I found you a cook."

Joe laughed. Lucinda stiffened, tried to pull free, but he wouldn't let her.

"You found me a woman who needs to consult with Julia Childs before she can boil water."

"No! She learned to cook in Florence..."

"She doesn't know Florence from Florenze."

"Now you are confusing me, Joseph."

"Never mind." His eyes narrowed with anger. "The only thing this babe knows how to cook are testosterone levels."

"What?"

"The little lady here spends her evenings entertaining gentlemen."

Nonna clapped a hand to her heart. *"Dio mio,"* she whispered.

"It isn't true," Lucinda said quickly. "I don't do anything of the sort, Mrs. Romano, your grandson is—"

"And," Joe said triumphantly, "to top it all, she's not even Italian. How's that grab you, Nonna, my love?"

Tears glittered in Nonna's eyes. "But you said," she whispered to Lucinda, "you said your name was—"

"Lucinda Barry. From the Boston Barrys." Lucinda blinked. Had she really said that? It was the first time in her life she'd fallen back on the horrid phrase, but right now, it was all she had.

"So, that's the story," Joe said. "She can't cook. She's not Italian. And she not only likes men, she loves 'em." He beamed a smile at Lucinda. The sight of it sent a chill coursing through her blood. She tried to move away from him but his arm clamped even more tightly around her. "And, you know what, Nonna dearest?"

"What?" Nonna whispered.

"I've decided, despite everything, you finally made the right choice."

His grandmother stared at him as if he'd lost his mind, and hell, maybe he had, but it was too good to pass up. Revenge, he thought, revenge so swift and sweet that when it was over, his dear, devoted, irritating-as-hell Nonna would never, ever try and play matchmaker again.

Joe put his hand under Lucinda's chin and lifted her startled face to his.

"I've finally realized that a man would be a fool to walk away from the right woman, once he's found her."

"What right woman?" Nonna said blankly, and he grinned.

"Why, this one," he purred, grinning at Lucinda. "The one you personally selected for me, Nonna, darling. Miss Lucinda-of-the-Boston-Barrys."

There was a moment of silence. Then his grandmother moaned, Lucinda gasped, and Joe used the moment to his advantage.

He bent his head, took Lucinda's mouth with his, and kissed her.

CHAPTER SEVEN

THE kiss was payback.

It was supposed to be, anyway.

An announcement that would set his grandmother back on her heels. A kiss that would show Lucy who was in charge here. All in all, a moment's revenge on two women who'd made his day a misery.

Except, it wasn't happening the way Joe had intended. Not once his mouth found Lucy's.

The kiss should have been a joke, not something he felt right down to his toes. The sweetness of her mouth. The warmth of her breath, as she gave a startled gasp. The softness of her body, as he drew her closer...

"Hey!"

The sharp bite of her teeth, as she sank them into his lip.

Joe jumped back, slapped his hand to his mouth, then looked at his fingers, smeared with pinpricks of bright red blood.

"You bit me," he said in amazement.

"You're damned right, I bit you!" Lucy's breasts rose and fell in rapid rhythm. "You—you—"

"Be careful what you call my Joseph," Nonna said.

Lucy swung towards the old woman. "Your Joseph," she said hotly, "is a no-good, no-account, lying, cheating, miserable son of a—"

"My Joseph has a poor sense of humor," Nonna said coldly. "Isn't that right, Joey?" She turned towards him, her expression beseeching, her voice turning soft and sweet. "It was a joke, yes? About you and this—this woman."

Joe looked from his grandmother's worried face to Blondie's indignant one. Now was the moment. Of course, he'd say, what else could it have been? Certainly, it was a joke, and in the

95

future, his nonna had better keep it in mind because if she meddled again…

But she *would* meddle again. A week from now, this would all be history. Give her a month, she'd be up to her elbows in more matchmaking.

"Joseph?"

Joe took a deep breath. "No," he said carefully. "It's not a joke. I'm going to marry Lucinda Barry."

His grandmother stared at him through dark, moist eyes and clapped a hand to her heart.

"No," she whispered, "oh, Joseph, *mio ragazzo,* no!"

"Oh, yes," he said politely. "Just consider, Nonna, and you'll see that she'll make me the perfect wife."

"This woman?" Nonna said, with a cold glare in Lucinda's direction. "One who is not Italian? Who cannot cook?"

"She can learn. " He smiled. "We can train her, darling Nonna. Together, we can make a silk purse from the proverbial sow's ear."

"I am *not* a sow's ear," Lucinda said furiously, "and you can stuff your silk purse!"

Joe ignored her. "As for her, uh, her talents with men…" He shrugged lazily. "You have to admit, Nonna, a woman well-versed in pleasing a man can be an asset."

"Are you two crazy? I don't want to be an asset! I am not marrying your grandson, Mrs. Romano. Have you got that straight?"

"At least, we agree on something! My Joseph deserves better."

"What your Joseph deserves," Lucinda said hotly, "is a good, swift kick! He's a horrible man."

"He is a saint."

"He's a pig."

"He is the heart of my heart."

"He's the devil incarnate! "

"Joseph," Nonna whispered imploringly, "tell me you are not really going to…oh, I cannot say the words!"

Joe shot his grandmother a quick, assessing look. Her voice trembled but her color was good and the hand she'd clapped over her heart was steady. Her sensibilities were wounded, that was all. His threat had hit her right where she lived, straight in her impossible, Old Country, matchmaking heart.

Good, he thought coolly, and reached for Lucinda again. She squirmed like a fish trying to avoid the hook but he drew her into the circle of his arm and held her there.

"Would I joke about such a thing?"

"I hope so."

"Nonna, sweetheart." He gave a rueful sigh. "I'm disappointed you'd have such an attitude towards my future bride."

Nonna moaned. Blondie made a choked little gasp that he figured would be acceptable to the New England WASP she claimed to be and bared her teeth. Joe, remembering their sharpness, maintained just the right distance.

"Joseph, I know you're upset but you cannot mean this. You cannot possibly marry such a woman."

"No, he cannot," Lucy snapped, and then she paused and fixed Nonna with a narrowed stare. "What do you mean, he can't marry such a woman?" Her lower lip, which had been trembling, fixed in a belligerent pout. "I'll have you know, Mrs. Romano, that I am not 'such a woman.' I am a fine woman, far too good for the likes of your awful grandson."

"My Joseph is a wonderful man," Nonna said hotly. "He deserves a woman who is a woman, not a—a—"

"I *am* a woman who is a woman," Lucy said just as hotly.

"You like men."

"Yes, I do. I mean, no. No, I don't. Not the way you mean."

"You cannot cook. And you are not Italian."

"I have a certificate from the culinary institute, and what's so special about being Italian?" Lucy glared at Joe. "Will you let go of me, dammit?"

Nonna made the sign of the cross. "She curses, too," she whispered. "Oh, Joseph. Tell me you won't do this."

Slowly, Joe let go of Lucy's arm and looked at his grandmother. Chance number two to say, of course he wouldn't...but then he remembered the day he'd just put in, thanks to this innocent-looking old lady with the braided coronet and the big, dark eyes. His stomach was so empty, it rumbled. His kitchen was a shambles, and had almost burned down around his ears. Worst of all, he'd been seduced into making an ass of himself in that torrid little skin-on-skin en-counter with Ms. Lucinda Barry, because what had happened had certainly been her doing, not his.

And why? Because his grandmother couldn't stop meddling in his love life, that was why. Well, enough was enough. Joe wasn't a gambler in the traditional sense of the word but he'd gotten what he had by knowing when to hold his cards and when to fold them.

Now was not the time to fold.

"You wanted me to find a wife," he said calmly.

His grandmother wiped her eyes with the skirt of her apron, looked at him beseechingly.

"I know, darling *Giuseppe,* but not a girl like this."

"A girl like what?" he said innocently, and looked over her shoulder.

The front door was open and the lady in question was gone.

Joe muttered an oath, kissed his grandmother's forehead, told her to concentrate on all the cute little non-Italian babies she'd soon have tumbling around her feet and on what fun it would be for her to do all the cooking for his family because, obviously, his wife would never be capable of producing a meal.

Nonna's cry of anguish almost stopped him, but memories of Miss Eyebrow and the teenybopper dragged him back to reality.

"I love you, Nonna, despite yourself," he said severely, though he softened things a bit with another peck on the cheek before he hurried out the door.

There was no sign of Lucy in the street. Joe cursed, revved up the Ferrari, winced at the sound of mashing gears and headed back towards the main street, the route they'd taken to get here.

Yes, there she was, determinedly puffing up the hill a couple of blocks away. Her hair had come loose and trailed down her back; somehow, she'd managed to lose one of those sensible shoes. Her blouse was still buttoned wrong, one side still hanging at half-mast.

Oh, yes. The neat little world Ms. Barry had built on a pack of lies—with the help of a meddlesome grandma—was coming apart. And she had the audacity to behave as if he were the bad guy!

Joe pulled closer to the curb and put down the window.

"Get in the car."

Blondie didn't answer. She didn't even look at him, or slow her pace.

His jaw tightened.

"I said, get in the damned car!"

"Go to hell," she said, and quickened her pace.

Joe slammed the engine into neutral, got out, and grabbed her. She shrieked as he tossed her over his shoulder and marched back to his car. A couple out walking their poodle stopped and gaped in astonishment.

"Help," Lucinda screamed.

"Lover's quarrel," Joe said with a smile that was all teeth. He dumped her, unceremoniously, into the passenger seat and drove off.

To her credit, Blondie didn't do any more yelling or shouting. She simply sat beside him, ramrod-straight. He could almost feel the ice cubes forming in the air but that was better than it turning blue.

For a woman who claimed to be a Boston Brahmin, Ms. Barry had an interesting vocabulary.

Joe's eyes narrowed.

She was probably as much a blueblood as he was. The lady was a stripper, plain and simple, albeit one with an interesting facility for creating stories about herself.

He glanced over at her, taking in the tense profile, the folded arms, the dopey outfit.

Oh, yes, he thought grimly. Miss Lucinda Barry, of the Boston Barrys, was getting exactly what she deserved.

Joe pulled into his garage. Blondie got out of the car, slammed the door hard enough to rattle the dashboard, and strode through the door that connected to the kitchen. Once inside, she swung towards him.

"If you try to touch me," she said, "I swear, Romano, I'll kill you."

He believed her. The look in her eyes said it all.

"Baby, you're breaking my heart." Her fists came up as he reached out, but he easily avoided her flailing hands, clasped her shoulders and moved her aside. "Does this mean you're not pleased with our engagement?" he said as he tossed his keys on the counter.

"Engagement?" He heard the hiss of her breath as he headed down the hall, then the slap-slip of one sensible shoe and one bare foot as she hurried after him. "I'd sooner be engaged to an ax murderer!"

"Trust me, Blondie. The feeling is mutual."

He turned and looked at Lucy, his eyes hard, and she could see that he meant it. But she'd figured he hadn't meant what he'd said about marrying her. Of course he hadn't, and a damned good thing, too.

"I only said that for my grandmother's benefit."

She watched as he leaned back against the staircase banister and tucked his hands into the pockets of his jeans. The snug, faded denim tightened across his hips and thighs. Oh, it was definitely a good thing he hadn't meant it. What woman would let a man force her into marrying a macho, arrogant, stubborn, oversexed, under-brained stud? Certainly, not her. Not her, even if that first touch of his lips on hers, after he'd made his incredible announcement, had almost stopped her heart…

"After this, the old girl won't dare interfere in my love life again."

What a smug, self-satisfied expression the man had on his face. Lucinda lifted her chin.

"I see," she said coldly. "You decided to administer shock treatment to your own grandmother."

"Something like that."

"With me as the source of the current."

He grinned. "Uh-huh."

"Your grandmother loves you."

"Of course she does."

"And yet, you'd treat her this way?"

"Like you said, Blondie, it's shock treatment."

"Don't call me that!"

"Sorry, honey."

"Don't call me that, either. I am not your 'honey.'"

"Well, what else would a man call his fiancée. Baby? Darling? Sweetie?" One dark brow lifted. "You don't strike me as the 'Lambykins' type."

"I am not your type at all, Romano. And I am, most definitely, not the type of woman who enjoys being used."

"Out of bed, you mean."

The drawled words were insolent but Lucinda knew there was no sense in letting him draw her into a discussion about her morals, or the supposed lack of them.

"Did it ever occur to you," she said, "that I might not enjoy being part of your nasty little scheme?"

"It isn't nasty, it's necessary. And no, it didn't occur to me. Not in the slightest. Why would it, when you're as much to blame for this nonsense as my grandmother?"

"My God, you're a horrible man!"

"So you keep telling me."

A moment passed. Then Lucinda folded her arms. "Well?" Joe folded his, too. "Well, what?"

"You made your point. Your grandmother believed you."

"So?"

"So, aren't you going to phone her and tell her it was all a hoax?"

"A lesson, not a hoax." Joe lifted one hand, checked his nails, flashed a seemingly lazy smile. "Either way, I'm not calling her yet."

"Fine." Lucinda started past him. "That's your business. She's your grandmother and it's your life, and it doesn't matter to me one little bit how you—"

His hand clamped around her wrist. "Just where do you think you're going?"

"Upstairs to pack." She smiled tightly. "I know this will come as a shock, Romano, but I'm leaving."

"No." Joe's tone was still pleasant, almost thoughtful. "No, you're not."

"I most certainly am. And you'd better let go of my wrist."

"You really think that's it?" Joe didn't ease his grip on her. If anything, he tightened his hold and moved closer, so close that she had to tilt her head back to meet his eyes. "You use my innocent grandmother to set up a scam—"

"Innocent?" Lucinda laughed. "She's as innocent as a used car salesman."

"And you'd probably know all about used car salesmen, new car salesmen, out-of-town salesmen, hell, salesmen in general. Wouldn't you, honey?"

"Let go of me, dammit!"

"You used her, so you could invade my home—"

"Invade your...? Oh, please! What are you, huh? One of those conspiracy nuts?"

"—invade my home, damn near incinerate it, and now you think you're going to pack your G-string and sashay off into the night?"

"For the thousandth time, I don't have a— Oh, what's the difference?" Lucinda blew a strand of hair off her forehead. "Yes, that's precisely what I'm going to do. Pack my G-string, walk out of this insane asylum and pretend I never met anybody named 'Romano.'"

"So, you admit it."

"That you Romanos are crazy?"

"That you do what I said you do, for a living."

Their eyes met, his as coldly blue as the sky on a midwinter morning. Of course not, she thought of saying. I don't do those things. I never even knew anybody really *did* do those things, until last night.

But why should she defend herself to this man? She'd already done that, almost begged him to believe her, and where had it gotten her? No place, that was where. Not that she cared. Mr. Almighty Romano was nothing in her life. An hour from now, she probably wouldn't even be able to conjure up his face.

To hell with explanations and with him, Lucinda thought, and tugged her hand free.

"I don't have to answer to you or anybody else." Her voice was icy and calm. She hoped so, anyway. "My life, and my choices, are my own."

"Why?" A muscle knotted in his jaw. He stepped closer; despite herself, she stepped back but her spine hit the banister. There was nowhere to go, no choice but to face him down. "Why?" he repeated, his voice low and rough. "If you can make your own choices, why choose to flaunt yourself in front of men?"

Color stole into Lucinda's cheeks. "I just told you, I don't owe you any explanations, Romano. My life—"

"Is your own. Yeah, so you said." The muscle danced in his jaw again, flickering tightly just beneath his skin. "Is it because you get a kick out of turning men on?"

"That's none of your business."

"It sure as hell is. You made it my business, lying your way in here."

Lucinda rolled her eyes. "Are we back to that? I didn't lie. I didn't do anything but accept a job—a job your sainted grandmother offered to me."

"Leave her out of this."

"I'll be happy to leave all of you out of this. Just let me get up the stairs. Five minutes from now, you'll never know I was here."

"Does it give you a kick?" Joe reached out, touched a callused finger to her cheek. She flinched back but the tip of his finger stayed, slowly following the line of her cheek down to her throat. "Flaunting yourself in front of strangers, I mean. Exhibiting yourself that way."

"Yes," she said, slapping angrily at his hand. "That's right. It gives me a kick, knowing men like you won't ever get the chance to do anything but watch me—what did you call it? Sashay around in my G-string?" Her smile glittered. "You can look, Romano, but you can't touch. That's what turns me on."

The change that came over him was swift and frightening.

His features hardened, and she knew, instantly, she'd pushed him too far.

"You're a liar," he said, and before she could protest, he reached for her and drew her towards him.

Her heart thudded.

"Stop it!" She grasped his arms, tried to hold herself rigid, but he was far too strong. Inexorably, inch by inch, he pulled her closer until she was pressed against him. His body was hard, powerfully male; she could feel his swift arousal nudging her belly and her pulse began to race. "Romano, you're not going to prove anything by acting like a thug—"

"Maybe flaunting yourself for men who can look but not touch turned you on in the past." His smile was quick and dangerous. "But that isn't what turned you on in my arms this morning."

"That," she said, trying to sound scornful.

"Yeah," he said roughly, "that."

His hand swooped down, cupped her breast. His thumb rolled lightly across the center and instantly, before she could draw a breath, she felt herself ignite, felt her nipple bead and harden under that insolent caress.

"You see?" His other arm swept around her, his hand splaying in the small of her back, and he pulled her tightly against him. "You can't hide what you feel, Blondie. What I make you feel."

"You're wrong." Her throat was dry; she could feel the breath rasp in her lungs but she forced herself to look up at him and meet his eyes with her own. "It was an act, Romano. Acting as if I'm turned on is what I do, remember? And I'm good at it."

"I'll bet you are, honey." His smile was quick and knowing. "But the heat of your skin was real. So was the way your mouth trembled under mine."

"I told you, it was—"

She cried out as he dipped his head and bit gently at her bottom lip.

"You were wet for me," he whispered. "Wet, and hot, and ready…"

"That's a lie," she said as he cupped the back of her head with his hand, "dammit, it's—"

Whatever she'd been going to say was lost against his mouth as it closed over hers.

His determination was reflected in his kiss. His mouth took. Demanded. Sought dominance, and offered nothing in return. Lucinda tried to twist her face from Joe's. She struggled. She fought...

And his kiss changed.

He angled his mouth over hers; his lips softened and clung. They moved against hers, brushed hers like satin whispering over silk.

Don't respond, she told herself, oh, don't. She was being kissed by a man who knew all there was to know about women. This was seduction, nothing else, an exercise designed to prove his mastery of her.

Don't, she thought again...and sighed against his mouth.

Joe slid his hand down her spine, then up, curved his fingers around the nape of her neck, tilting her head back. His other arm tightened around her. He held her as if she were something precious. As if she were the only woman he'd ever wanted.

As if she'd been meant only for this moment, and for him.

He made a sound, something between a groan of anguish and one of need. His mouth brushed hers again with light, feathering strokes; his teeth teased the fullness of her bottom lip.

"Lucy," he whispered, "open for me."

She told herself he was crazy. That she'd never kiss him that way.

But she did. She parted her lips, let him dip his tongue into her mouth, and the taste of him filled her.

Someone moaned. Someone whimpered. Was it she? Lucinda didn't know. She couldn't think, didn't want to think. She only wanted the kiss never to end as she wound her arms around Joe's neck and kissed him back.

He said something. She couldn't understand it—were the words Italian? But oh, she understood the way he lifted her to him. The way he slid his hands down her sides, caught her skirt and raised it. She felt the slide of his rough fingers against her naked flesh. Felt the rush of hot, wet heat that gathered between her thighs.

Lucinda gasped. She shifted her weight. She hadn't intended to do that, hadn't meant to lean into him…

Don't lie to yourself, Lucinda.

That was just what she'd intended. She wanted this. All of it. Joe's arms, holding her tight. His erection, hard against her belly. The whisper of his breath on her mouth, the taste of him on her lips. The feel of his fingers there, yes, there, just there, teasing her.

Most of all, she wanted him.

Now. Right now. Right here. Their clothes, lying tangled on the floor. His arms, lifting her, carrying her to the sofa. His weight, bearing her down.

"Joe," she whispered, "Joe, please…"

And he dropped his arms to his sides and let go of her.

For a moment, for an eternity, Lucinda was too stunned to understand what had happened. She only knew that she'd lost the hard support of Joe's body; the protection of his embrace.

"Please, what?"

His tone was polite, as if he'd asked her the time of day. She blinked her eyes, forced them open. Her legs felt as if they were going to buckle and she staggered, clutched the banister behind her…

And saw Joe, standing very still, his eyes locked to her face.

A terrible coldness swept through her bones.

Once, a long time ago, she'd gone walking near a salt marsh back home in Massachusetts. She'd noticed a dark splotch on the dead limb of a pine tree. At closer range, she'd recognized it as a bird. A hawk of some kind, its unwavering gaze fixed on something in the distance.

The "something" had turned out to be a rabbit feeding in the grass. The little creature never had a chance. A flap of those great wings, a swoop, a flurry of claws and fur, and the rabbit was no longer a rabbit.

Had it felt, in its last few seconds, as betrayed as she felt now?

"You see?" Joe's voice was cool, calm, almost serene. "You were wrong, Lucy. I do turn you on. And I could have you, if I wanted you." A smile twisted across his face. "But I don't. And that means you lose, baby. Whatever you hoped for, you're not going to get it. No easy score. No rich boyfriend or maybe even a husband to snare, thanks to the foolishness of an old woman." The smile came again, and a lift of his eyebrows. "What's the matter, honey? Run out of names to call me?"

Lucinda told herself not to let him see what he'd done to her. Every word, every action, would count if she were to salvage even a crumb of pride. Carefully, she drew herself up. And she smiled, too, as brightly as he.

"Why would I call you anything, Mr. Romano, when you're so certain you have all the answers?" She turned, started up the stairs. She could feel his gaze on her and she steeled herself not to look back until she was sure the moment was right. "But you don't," she said, and swung towards him. "Not if you think that little performance just now was all yours."

She had the pleasure of seeing the smile slip from Joe's handsome face. His eyes grew dark; his mouth thinned, and he started towards the stairs.

"Liar," he growled.

Lucinda turned and fled.

Joe sat at his desk in the library of his house in Pacific Heights, and waited.

Five minutes, maybe ten, had passed. There'd been no sound from upstairs, except for the slam of Lucy's door.

Now, he was waiting for her to come down the stairs, exit his home and his life. Once she did, he'd phone his grandmother, tell her the stuff about taking Lucinda Barry as his wife had all been nonsense, give her a stern lecture about interfering in his affairs.

In other words, his life could go back to normal.

Damned right, it would.

Joe huffed out a breath, shoved back his chair and got to his feet. As it was, this nonsense had wasted far too much of his time. It was Saturday. He had things to do on Saturday. Get ready for Saturday night, for one. He had a date tonight, with that redhead he'd met at the art show in Ghiardelli Square on Wednesday. Hadn't he said he'd give her a call, tell her what time he'd be picking her up for dinner?

For dinner, where? That new place in Chinatown? Or maybe that restaurant on the wharf. Yeah. They did great lobster, even better shrimp.

He could imagine what his new cook would do if she found a lobster on the counter. Or a batch of raw shrimp. Scream, probably, when she saw those beady black eyes. Those feathery tentacles...

Joe frowned.

What in hell did he care what she'd think or do? Lucinda Barry wasn't his cook. She wasn't anybody's cook. And she wasn't his problem, either.

He went back to his desk, reached for the phone and his address book. He'd call the redhead first, then the restaurant for reservations. What was her name? Something Lee. Kimber-lee. Bever-lee. Sara—

Joe's stomach rumbled.

When was the last time he'd eaten? That was a better question. Sometime last night. That awful stuff at the bachelor party, just after Blondie had popped from the cake. The closest he'd come to anything even resembling food since then was this morning, when she'd incinerated breakfast. How could a woman ruin bacon and eggs? Even he could manage them, and he was no cook.

Yeah, he thought grimly, and neither was she. She was a scheming piece of fluff who could drive a man crazy, if a man was foolish enough to let that happen. Well, he wasn't. He'd agreed to take on a cook, not a courtesan.

The sooner the woman was out of his house and out of his life, the better.

What was taking her so long?

Joe shot an angry look at the still-empty hallway. Then he opened his address book and started thumbing through it. Marilee. That was the redhead's name, and there was her phone number. He punched it in, impatiently counted off three rings before a sultry voice said hello.

The tension began easing from his body. That hello told him everything he needed to know. Marilee wouldn't bite a man's head off.

She wouldn't walk around in a shapeless skirt and blouse when he knew there was a body that wouldn't quit hiding beneath it.

She wouldn't wear her hair skinned back from her ears when he knew those golden tresses could spill like silk through a man's hands.

And she damned well wouldn't pretend her response to him was all an act because the truth was, he had only to touch her to make her moan with desire...

"Hell," Joe snarled, and slammed down the phone.

He shot to his feet, dug his hands into his pockets and stalked from one end of the room to the other.

"It's an act, pal," he muttered. "That's all it is. Little Miss Sunshine turns into a seductress when it suits her. And vice versa. Who knows what she's up to? Who knows..."

Footsteps sounded in the hall. Joe pulled the door open. Lucinda—and who did she think she was kidding with that name?—Lucinda stood at the foot of the steps, her suitcase at her feet.

He thought of telling her that she should have asked him to carry it down. He thought of telling her she had a hell of a nerve to have pushed her way into his life. He thought of walking straight to where she stood, plucking the pins from that ridiculous chignon and stripping her out of the Mary Poppins costume...

"I'm leaving," she said.

"I'm delighted to hear it."

He certainly didn't look delighted. He was glowering, his mouth was tightly compressed, and his arms were folded over his chest. Still, Lucinda knew what he meant because she felt the same way.

If she never saw Joe Romano again, it would be too soon.

First, though, there was a small, uncomfortable scene to play out. It was what had taken her so long. Packing had been a five-minute affair because she'd been too angry to bother folding things neatly. Instead, she'd dumped everything out of the drawers, off the hangers, and into her suitcases. Then she'd picked up her purse…and realized she'd spent most of her last twenty dollars this morning, for the taxi that had brought her here.

In other words, her capital consisted of the change from that twenty and the emergency pair of ten dollar bills she kept tucked in her wallet.

She was broke.

She'd taken all of it—the couple of single bills and the tens—smoothed them out and put them into her change purse, as if it might look like more that way. It hadn't. Her knees had gone weak at the thought of being virtually penniless in San Francisco—and then she'd remembered that she'd put in a day, one long and horrible day, as Joe Romano's employee.

He owed her a paycheck.

Asking him for it would be the final humiliation, but if there was one thing the past months had taught her, it was that you did what you had to do, to survive.

Remember that, she told herself, and cleared her throat.

"Mr. Romano."

A taunting smile tilted at the corner of his mouth. "I see we've returned to formal mode."

"Mr. Romano, you owe me money."

"Excuse me?"

"I worked here for—" Lucinda looked at her watch "—for almost seven hours. Pro-rating my salary by the hour, that means—"

"You did what, Ms. Barry?"

Lucinda flushed. The bastard was going to make her beg.

"I put in seven hours as your employee. That means you owe me—"

"We seem to have a communications problem." Lazily, Joe uncoiled from the doorway, tucked his hands into the back pockets of his jeans and strolled towards her. "You used the word 'work.'"

"That's correct. You hired me at eight this morning. You fired me at three this afternoon. And——"

"You told me you were my new cook at eight this morning." His smile didn't quite reach his eyes. "I didn't check the clock but it wasn't much later than that when you tried to set fire to the kitchen."

"That is not true!"

"Then I discovered your qualifications were phony and took you to my grandmother's, where your little scheme unraveled like a ball of twine rolling down a staircase." Joe folded his arms again and arched an eyebrow. "Where, if you don't mind my asking, does the concept of 'work' enter into the scenario?"

Lucinda knew she was blushing. And that she was painfully close to marching up to him, slapping that contemptuous smirk from his handsome face and telling him, in excruciating detail, exactly what he could do with the money he owed her.

Instead, she lifted her chin another notch.

"There's nothing to debate, Mr. Romano. You hired me, you fired me, and you owe me a day's wages." Unhesitatingly, she stuck out her hand. A piece of paper lay in it. The paper trembled, which she figured spoiled the effect, but she was undaunted. "Here's the amount. Check it, by all means, but you'll find it accurate."

Joe peered at the paper in her outstretched palm.

"I'm sure it is," he said politely, lifting his eyes to hers. "What's inaccurate, however, is your conviction that I'm going to pay you for the time you spent in my home."

"Pay me," Lucinda said quickly, as he started to turn away, "or I'll sue you."

That stopped him. He swung towards her, head cocked as if he hadn't heard her right. "Excuse me?"

"I said, I'll sue you for the money."

"*You'll* sue *me* for…?" Joe chuckled. The chuckle became a laugh, the laugh a guffaw. "Oh, hell," he said, and slapped his thigh, "this is wild! You're going to sue me for wages you didn't earn?"

"A matter of opinion. Mr. Romano. I think I did earn them, and I suspect a judge will, too."

He looked at her. She looked at him. Joe's smile slipped. Damned if she wouldn't do it. He could just see her marching into small claims court, looking prim and proper, suing him for what amounted to what he'd have spent on a couple of bottles of good wine.

The tabloids would love the story. So would his business adversaries. And when it came out, as it surely would, that Lucinda the Cook was really Blondie the Stripper...

Joe gave a throaty growl, dug out his wallet and handed her some bills.

"That's too much. If you check my math—"

"Just keep the change."

Lucinda shook her head, opened her pocketbook, then her purse. She dug inside, and took out a ten dollar bill, two quarters and a dime.

"I only want what's coming to me," she said, holding it out to him.

Her hand was shaking. He'd thought so, before, when she'd first extended it. Now, he was sure of it. Well, so what? So her hand shook. What of it? She was nervous. And she should be.

"Take the money, please."

Joe rolled his eyes and did as she'd asked. Anything to get her out the door.

"Thank you."

"You're welcome."

"I'll send for my kitchen things some other time."

"Fine."

He watched as she hoisted the suitcase. The muscle in his jaw knotted and unknotted. The damned thing was heavy; he'd felt its weight this morning. And he could see the strain showing in the bowing of her shoulders.

Oh, for God's sake...

"Just give me that," he snapped, but Lucinda tugged it out of reach when he tried to grab the handle.

"I don't need your help."

"Think of it this way, Ms. Barry. You trip, hurt yourself carrying this lump of lead, and you'll undoubtedly sue me." His smile was quick and unpleasant. "It's in my interest to take it out to the taxi for you."

A soft wash of pink rose in her face. "I didn't call for a taxi."

"Well, you should have." Why didn't the woman stand still instead of dancing away from him with her luggage? "There's no public transportation near this house."

"I like to walk."

"You'll be walking all night, just trying to get downtown. Dammit," Joe said, and made another grab. "Will you stand—"

The suitcase went flying. So did her pocketbook, which spilled open. Lucinda's change purse burst open, and her money flew across the floor. She shot Joe a mortified look, went down on her knees to gather it up, but he beat her to it and scooped up the bills.

Aside from what he'd just given her, she had less than fourteen dollars.

Joe looked at her. "Where's the rest of your money?"

Lucinda felt her cheeks turn hot. "In your hand."

"That's all of it?"

She didn't reply.

He frowned. "Fourteen bucks is all you've got? That, plus what I just gave you?"

"What you just *paid* me," she said with dignity. "Give it to me, please."

"This won't even cover a cab ride to the nearest bank machine."

Lucinda reached for her money. Joe closed his fist tight.

"You do have an ATM card, don't you?"

Her color deepened. "Of course." It wasn't a lie. She had one. Unfortunately, the account it had once accessed was empty.

Joe got to his feet. She did, too. "I don't believe you."

"Romano, I don't care what you believe." Lucinda made a

grab for his hand, but he lifted it over his head. "That's my money! Hand it over."

"You're broke," he said flatly.

"My finances are not your concern."

She was right. They weren't. She wasn't. And he had no doubt that a babe as clever as this one wouldn't stay broke for long. San Francisco was full of clubs, and private parties, and men who'd pay damned near anything for the pleasure of watching her take down all that soft, golden hair and turn from a schoolmarm into a seductress.

Joe felt as if somebody had kicked him right where he lived.

"You're right," he said. "They aren't." He reached for her suitcase, snatched it up, and headed for the stairs. "But a man in my position can't afford gossip."

Lucinda stared after him. He was going up the steps like a whirlwind, and now he was making his way down the hall.

"What are you doing? Romano! Romano…"

He didn't answer. She mouthed a word she'd never realized she knew and flew after him.

"Are you crazy?" she said when he shouldered open the door to the room she'd just vacated and dumped her things on the bed. "I quit, remember?"

"You didn't."

"I did."

"I fired you." He turned to her, his expression grim, his hands on his hips. "You just said so. It's why I owed you a day's pay."

Lucinda stared at him. He *was* crazy. She told him so.

"You're crazy, if you think I'd stay in this house."

"You're crazier, if you think I'd let you wheedle out of a deal."

She blinked. "What deal?"

Joe's glower deepened. "I'm the employer here, Blondie. That means I get to ask the questions. Is there any possibility you can boil water?"

Her spine stiffened. "What a stupid question."

"Is that a yes?"

"Certainly, it's a yes."

"Can you use a can opener?"

Lucinda blew a strand of hair off her forehead. "I won't dignify that with a response."

"Is that another yes?" Joe snapped.

"I can also open jars of mayonnaise and cartons of milk," she said coldly. "And—surprise, surprise—in a pinch, I can even unwrap the plastic from a package of frozen hamburger."

"Done," Joe said, and marched past her to the door.

Bewildered, she spun towards him. "What's done?"

"You're hired. Rehired. Cook for me for the rest of the month, let my grandmother go on thinking you and I are an item, and I'll give you a month's severance pay on top of your salary. That's the deal."

She couldn't speak at all, she could only gape. "But—but—but—"

"I wanted to teach Nonna a lesson. Well, it won't be any kind of lesson at all if I only keep her dangling for a day."

"You can keep that poor old woman dangling forever, Romano. You certainly don't need me to do it."

"My nonna isn't stupid. She'll smell a rat, if you vanish now."

"And just what makes you think I'd go along with this insane plan of yours?"

"Four thousand bucks," Joe said brusquely, "that's what makes me think it."

Lucinda blanched. "Four thousand...?"

"I'll double your severance pay and give you room and board."

"Yes, but—"

"You might as well save your breath, Blondie." Joe folded his arms. Stony-faced, he stared at her. "I'm not about to go a penny higher. Now, is it a deal?"

"I—I..." Lucinda swallowed. "Yes," she said faintly. "It's a deal."

Joe nodded. "Good."

The door swung shut after him. Lucinda stared at it, shook her head, then wrenched it open. There had to be some rules, rules of her own making, so he'd know she wasn't spineless.

"Romano?"

He was halfway down the steps. At the sound of Lucy's voice, he stopped and looked up over his shoulder.

"Yeah?"

"You call me 'Blondie' again, I'll quit."

Her chin was trembling. Her eyes glittered suspiciously. Her hair looked as if she'd been caught in a wind tunnel and yet, for all of that, she almost radiated dignity.

"You quit, you won't get that money."

Lucy straightened her shoulders. "Money isn't everything."

But it was. To her, anyway. Otherwise, why did she dance for strangers? Why did she taunt them with that beautiful body? And why had she accepted a job in his home when she knew as much about cooking as he did about cardiac surgery?

The questions raced through Joe's head, but he didn't ask them. The answers were none of his business. Keeping his grandmother on tenterhooks for two weeks, was. And keeping his fake fiancée around was the best way to do that.

"Okay," he said, and shrugged. "No more Blondie."

"Good."

She shut the door. Joe thought about what it was going to be like to know she was sleeping in the room right next to his...

The lock clicked home. He let out his breath and went on down the stairs.

It wasn't until he was safely back in his library that he began to wonder just what he'd let himself in for.

CHAPTER EIGHT

WHAT did a man do when he had an unwanted woman in his house?

Okay, Joe thought as he lay wide awake in his bed hours later. Okay, so that wasn't exactly accurate.

Blondie was here at his request. They'd struck a deal, one that would benefit them both. He'd get the chance to teach his nonna a lesson. Blondie would get some much-needed cash...

But he wasn't going to call her that. Not anymore. She'd stood in that hallway, as desperate for money as a woman could possibly be, but her determination to face him down hadn't wavered.

"My name isn't Blondie," she'd said.

And he'd figured, okay, what was the harm in humoring her? Fine, he'd told her, he wouldn't call her that. He'd call her Lucinda.

"Lucinda," Joe muttered, and rolled his eyes.

What sort of name was that for a woman like her? A man thought of a Lucinda, he thought of high-necked blouses, not sequins and G-strings. Was it her real name, or was it part of her act? Drumroll, curtain up, spotlight...

And now, gentlemen, for your evening's pleasure, Miss Lucinda Barry...

Joe frowned and laced his hands beneath his head.

What she did, and who she did it with, wasn't his problem. Nothing about her was his problem. She'd cook his meals, after a fashion, for the next couple of weeks; she'd play at being his fiancée. In return, he'd given her a roof over her head. Soon enough, he'd write out a check, hand it over, and that would be that.

A deal was a deal. And, as deals went, this one was not just reasonable, it was a win-win situation, all the way around.

117

In which case, why was he lying here, every muscle tight as a coiled spring? Why were his eyelids all but pinned open at—he glanced at the clock on the nightstand and groaned—at almost 4:00 in the a.m. Why couldn't he stop imagining how Lucinda looked, asleep in the next room, her hair loose and spread out over the pillow, her lashes feathered against her cheeks?

Dammit, Joe thought. He sat up, grabbed his pillow, punched it into submission and lay down again.

"Get a grip, Romano," he said.

It wasn't as if he was desperate for a woman. On the contrary. He'd spent the evening with a woman he could have had for the asking. After he'd settled things with Blondie—with Lucinda—he'd called the redhead, picked her up at eight and taken her out to dinner. Then they'd gone on to a hole-in-the-wall club and listened to some great blues. He'd thought it was great; Red didn't seem to notice. But afterwards, on the dance floor, she'd melted against him like hot wax.

"I just love slow dancing," she'd sighed, and her pelvis had moved against his in the kind of vertical tango that would probably have been banned in Boston.

And, just that quickly, his thoughts had left the woman in his arms and flown across town to his house. To his guest room, and the woman inside it. His unwanted, unexpected cook *cum* fiancée *cum* general, all-purpose pain in the butt.

Was she still in her room, with the door shut and locked? he wondered. Would she be waiting to hear the sound of the garage door opening as he parked his car?

"I just love the sound of a saxophone," Red had purred, and he'd blinked, said something really brilliant like yeah, so did he. Then he'd all but dragged her off the tiny dance floor, paid the check, popped her into a cab along with a peck on the cheek, a twenty dollar bill for the fare, and a muttered excuse about having a headache...

A headache.

"Hot damn," Joe mumbled, and sat up.

Men didn't have headaches, for God's sake. Not him, anyway. Not ever, and certainly not the sort that would make him pass on the chance to spend the night with a beautiful, sexy, warm, willing lady.

Joe tossed back the covers and turned on the bedside lamp.

Lucinda hadn't been waiting. She probably didn't even know he'd been out. The house had been dark and silent; not even a sliver of light had spilled from under her door. He'd gone into his own room, peeled off his clothes, stepped into the shower and turned the spray to cold...

"This," Joe said aloud, "is ridiculous."

There was a blonde in the guest room. So what? He didn't even like blondes. Never had. Redheads had more fire. And this particular blonde, especially, had little to recommend her. One minute, she played at being a cold and proper Bostonian. The next, she sizzled in his arms, made him forget he was a civilized man, made him forget everything except the need to possess her, even though a hundred other men had been there before him and kissed that soft, hot mouth. Cupped those delicate breasts. Inhaled her scent, tasted her skin...

Joe cursed, strode into his bathroom and stepped into the shower.

Maybe he hadn't made such a good deal, after all.

Maybe this hadn't been such a good idea, after all.

Agreeing to Joe Romano's scheme had made sense. Well, Lucinda thought as she stared up at the ceiling over her bed, well, perhaps it hadn't really made sense. In truth, his plan was crazy, but that was just the point. It was *his* plan, not hers. If he thought he could teach his grandmother a lesson by pretending he was engaged to her, so be it. The whole thing would only last a few weeks. Nobody would get hurt, and she'd end up with enough cash to tide her over until she found a job.

Lucinda sighed and rolled onto her side.

If it was all that simple, why was she having such trouble falling asleep?

Because it rankled, that was why. Because it was insulting and humiliating and downright infuriating that Joe Romano should think she was so repugnant that he could get even with his grandmother just by saying he intended to marry her.

The whole thing was preposterous.

In real life, *she* was the one who would never consider marrying *him*.

Lucinda rolled onto her back.

The man obviously thought he was quite a catch. The sexy eyes. The dangerous smile. The boyish good looks and the hard-muscled body. The house on a hill in Pacific Heights and the city at his feet.

Oh, yes. Joe Romano man had a high opinion of himself. But could he trace his ancestors back to the *Mayflower*? Could he lay claim to a family tree that bristled with a bunch of names known to every American schoolchild?

Lucinda sat up, punched the pillows into place and folded her arms.

She could just imagine her mother's reaction if she announced she were engaged to Joe Romano. Why, her mother would probably gasp, just as Nonna Romano had this afternoon. She might even fall into a dead faint. Anyone could see a Romano wasn't equal to a Barry, not by a long shot.

He was too blunt. Too outspoken. Too rough and ready and altogether macho for his own good or anybody else's. And any idiot could tell he must have once worked with his hands, or else where would he get those muscles?

Those amazing muscles, that she'd felt under her hands when he'd taken her in his arms and kissed her. Kissed her, as if he'd never wanted a woman as much as he wanted her, as if nothing mattered but her, as if...

Lucinda frowned and switched on the bedside lamp. She pushed the blanket aside, got up and went to the dresser where she'd left her stash of cookbooks after she'd unpacked her things again.

This had been an upsetting day. She needed sleep, but it was obvious she wasn't going to get any. How could she possibly, when she'd made a deal with the devil himself?

She was pretty sure she knew what Joe Romano thought, that she couldn't cook worth a lick but that he'd make up for a bad bargain by seducing her into his bed.

"Wrong on both counts, Romano," Lucinda said coldly.

Then she climbed back into bed, opened the book, and started reading.

Joe rose at six to gray skies and dreary rain.

He took a shower—his third since he'd gone to bed—and dressed quickly in an old U.C.L.A. sweatshirt with the sleeves cut out, gray running shorts, and high-top Nikes that had seen better days.

A glance in the mirror confirmed what he already suspected.

His eyes were bloodshot, his expression grim. He looked like a man who needed a good night's sleep and, dammit, he did. Each time he'd dozed off, he'd dreamed about the blonde in the next bedroom, dreams that had sent him to the shower stall until, by now, his fingertips were starting to look like prunes.

But the dreams were gone, and for good.

The last one had done it.

He'd dreamed he was in a big room filled with salesmen. Old ones, young ones, car salesmen, drapery salesmen, pharmaceutical salesmen, all kinds of salesmen, all of them seated in a big circle, chanting, "Lu-cin-da. Lu-cin-da."

A bolt of lightning had sizzled from the ceiling straight down into the center of that circle and ignited a puff of white smoke. And when the smoke cleared, there was Lucinda, dressed in a white chef's cap, a frilly white apron, a pair of sensible white shoes and nothing else.

"Hi, boys," she'd purred. "It's time to turn up the heat and start cooking."

The men had cheered, Lucinda had laughed, and somewhere in the distance a fire alarm had started to wail. Joe had shot up in bed, awakening from sleep with a pounding heart and a pounding head. He'd taken one last cold shower and while he stood under the spray, it had occurred to him that this dream would be his last.

His subconscious was smarter than his libido. It knew that Blondie—and hell, that was still what he was going to call her, whether she liked it or not—it knew that Blondie was nothing special.

And, at last, his libido knew it, too.

No more dreams, Joe thought as he left his room. No more cold showers. No more wanting a woman he didn't want to want...

"Good morning."

Her voice was polite, matter-of-fact, and so unexpected that he barely had time to glimpse Lucinda standing at the bottom of the steps before he tripped over his own feet. He muttered an oath, recovered quickly, and managed to make it down the last few steps without killing himself.

"Sorry. I didn't mean to startle you."

"You didn't," Joe said, lying through his teeth.

Of course, she'd startled him. What man expected to find the subject of his overheated dreams standing in his foyer at six-something in the morning, all decked out in an outfit that made her look like a cross between Dr. Frankenstein and the guy who tossed the dough at Sal's Pizzeria back in the old neighborhood?

What *was* she wearing? A white dress and a white jacket, both starched so stiff they probably could have stood upright by themselves. White stockings, those sensible white shoes. She even had on a hat. A tall hat. A...

"It's called a toque," she said, touching her hand to her head.

Joe blinked. Had he asked? He didn't think so, but—

"You were staring at my hat." Lucinda cleared her throat. "People sometimes do. I mean, they find these hats strange..."

"No," Joe said, and cleared his throat, too. "No, not at all."

Lucinda nodded and folded her hands at her waist. "I thought it best if I looked professional."

"Uh-huh."

"In case any of your friends should drop by, or anything."

At six in the morning? On a Sunday? "Oh, right. Right."

"I mean, it's one thing for your grandmother to think that we're, uh, that... You know. But other people should be aware that I am your cook."

"My cook," Joe repeated, and blanked his mind to yesterday's eggs. "Uh, right, right. But, the thing is, I'm going for a run. It's, ah, it's very early…"

"I know. But I remembered you liked to run, so I set my alarm clock for five-thirty."

"Your alarm clock." So that was what he'd heard, cutting through his heavy-duty dream.

"Yes." She smiled politely. "I wanted to get a head start on breakfast."

Breakfast. Oh, hell, breakfast.

"I see," he said politely. "But, uh, the thing is, I, uh, I…"

I, what? Improvise, improvise. Last evening, when he'd come up with this scheme, he'd told her he expected her to cook. But he didn't. Of course, he didn't. She couldn't cook; he knew that. The last thing he wanted this morning was to have to live through another session of burned bacon and raw eggs, or vice versa.

As for all those hot dreams… What hot dreams? Joe thought, and bit back a grin. What he'd felt—thought he'd felt—yesterday, had been an aberration. Seeing her in this ridiculous getup, he knew those dreams were most definitely history.

"And," he said with an equally polite smile, "I never eat before I run."

"No, of course not. My fiancé—"

"You have a *fiancé?*"

Lucinda shook her head. "No. Not anymore. But I did have. And he—"

"You were engaged. To be married."

"Yes." Her voice took on an edge, as did her smile. "Why are you so surprised, Mr. Romano?"

"I don't know. I thought…" What had he thought? What did he care if she'd had a dozen fiancés?

"Did you think a woman like me couldn't find a man who wanted to marry her?"

"Look, I'm just…" Joe ran a hand through his hair. "Never mind. Your personal life is none of my business."

"Exactly." She stepped back, her hands on her hips, her eyes cool. "I'll have breakfast waiting."

"No. No, thank you. Actually, Blon… I mean, actually,

Lucinda, I, ah, I've changed my mind about the cooking. It won't be nec—''

"It will."

"It won't. Just, uh, just posing as my fiancée will be sufficient."

"Just falling into your bed, you mean." She was on him in a second, jabbing a finger into his chest, fire flashing from her angry eyes to his bewildered ones. "Is that how you intend to have me earn my salary, Romano?"

"Yes," Joe said. He danced backwards, away from that finger and that furious glare. "I mean, no. I mean, I expect you to play the role you agreed to play."

"The deal was, I pretend to be your fiancée. And when I'm not pretending, I do the cooking. That's what I'm going to do. You got that?"

He looked down at her. Her hat had fallen over one eye. She looked enraged, silly, and almost incredibly beautiful.

"Romano? Do we understand each other?"

What he understood was that he ached to strip her out of that jacket and dress and make love to her here, right here, on the floor.

"Yes," he said, and he reached out, grasped her shoulders, put her aside and headed out the door without even pausing to do his warm-up stretches.

That was a mistake, yet one more error in a weekend's worth, he thought grimly as he pounded along the narrow, steep streets. A runner should always warm up first, just as a man should always weigh all the possibilities before entering into a business arrangement.

Joe paused at a red light and jogged in place.

His muscles were protesting being put to the test without advance notice but he could grit his teeth and run through the pain. It was the protests of his brain that were giving him the most trouble.

What on earth had he been thinking when he'd made that crazy deal with Lucinda?

The light changed. Joe ran across the street, up a hill, but halfway to the top, he turned and started down.

Okay. Enough was enough. He knew what Lucinda was, but he couldn't keep his hands off her. And she knew it. She was capitalizing on it. That outfit today, the no-nonsense chef's garb—why would she have worn it, except to drive his hormones wild? She had to know that all he could think about, when he saw her in that getup, was how she'd look out of it.

The minute he got home, the very second he came through the door, he'd get out his checkbook, write her a check for the amount they'd agreed on, and tell her she was free to go.

He'd deal with Nonna some other way. Some way that wouldn't keep him up nights and keep him torn between wanting to throttle his cookless cook and drag her off to bed.

Yes, he thought, and smiled as he let himself in the door, yes, his problem was solved. Solved, and painlessly...

Joe stopped, frowned and inhaled.

What was that smell?

It wasn't a bad smell. It wasn't a good smell. It was just...different. Sort of a cross between charred bacon and chocolate-chip cookies. No, no, it was more like, well, like chocolate. Chocolate, and bacon, and...

"Lucinda?"

And burning rubber, he thought as he raced to the kitchen.

"Lucinda? Blondie, are you..."

Oh, hell. Joe's heartbeat stumbled. The room was filled with smoke; the oven door stood open and he could see a thin layer of what looked like soot on the floor beneath it. He had a quick glimpse of a mountain of pots and pans, a sink filled with dishes, and then he was standing over Lucinda, who sat on a stool at the counter, her head—toque and all—buried in her arms.

"Blondie?" He grabbed for her, turned her towards him. The silly hat fell off as she lifted her eyes to his. His heart stumbled again as he saw the smudges on her cheeks, the wicked-looking slash of red above her lip. "Honey, what happened? Did you burn yourself?" Joe drew her off the stool and into his arms. "Just be calm. Don't get excited. Come with me, baby. I'll drive us straight to the emergency room."

"I did it," she said.

"Yes. I know you did." He slid his arm around her waist, kept his voice soft and low. "But it's okay, honey. You just need a couple of stitches to fix that cut."

"What cut?"

"The one over your mouth. Don't panic, Lucy. It's not a bad one."

Lucinda smiled, flicked out the tip of her tongue and licked at the red slash. "Raspberry," she said, and laughed.

Joe gaped. "Raspberry?"

"Mmm." She touched the tip of her finger to the red that remained, then held it out to him. "See?"

He looked at her finger, looked at her mouth. She brought her finger to his lip. Carefully, he tasted it.

"It is," he said slowly. "Raspberry, I mean."

"Of course." Lucinda smiled, put her hands on Joe's forearms, and looked up at him. "I made chocolate and raspberry pastries, Mr. Romano. For your breakfast."

Joe stared at her. "Chocolate and…"

"Uh-huh. Well, I suppose you really should call them *pain au chocolat,* for accuracy." Still smiling, she wriggled free of his arms, reached behind her and plucked something that looked like a disfigured oyster from the counter. "And I decided to experiment, to add some jam… What?"

"You mean," Joe said carefully, "this—this mess is the result of a session at the stove?"

"It's not a mess." Lucinda eyed the room. "Well, okay. Things look messy, but I haven't had the chance to clean up."

"You made a mess," Joe repeated, as if he were the King of Kitchen Cleanliness, "and you sat there and let me think you'd cut yourself, and all the time you knew it was nothing but a joke?"

Her smile faded. "My cooking is not a joke, Mr. Romano."

"A matter of opinion, Ms. Barry." Joe smiled thinly. "By the way, when did we revert back to formal address?"

"I thought it would be a good idea, now that we've agreed I'm to be your cook for the balance of the month."

"Ah. I see. You believe in getting into a part, is that right?"

Lucinda's gaze narrowed. His voice had gone cold, and there was a look about him that made her uneasy.

"Yes," she said, "yes, I do."

His smile was thin with undertones of danger. It sent her heart up into her throat.

"We also agreed that you would pretend to be my fiancée."

"I fail to see what that has to do with the present situation."

He failed to see it, either. All he knew was that this woman had, from the looks of it, almost burned his house down a second time, that she'd whipped up something inedible and expected him to get excited about it—and that she'd almost given him heart failure when he'd come running into the room, thinking she was hurt.

And then there was that swift, exciting taste of her flesh, when she'd put the tip of her finger to his mouth.

Joe took a slow step forward.

"It has everything to do with it," he said softly.

"It doesn't." Why was he looking at her that way? "There's no connection at all."

"There is." He moved closer. "You said you liked to get into a part."

"I didn't say that." Lucinda swallowed dryly. She wanted to put some distance between them but there was no place to go, not with the counter at her back. "Not exactly."

Joe reached out, put a hand on the counter on either side of her. "What did you say, exactly, Ms. Barry?"

"I said…" She caught her breath as he bent his head to hers and nuzzled the hair back from her ear. "What—what are you doing?"

"Smelling you." His voice was low and rough. The sound of it sent a tremor up her spine. "I like the way you smell, Lucy."

"My name is Lucinda."

"Lucy suits you." It did; how come he'd only just noticed that? "Mmm. What is that scent?"

"It's—it's vanilla. Or chocolate. Or—"

"It's flowers." Joe brushed his mouth against her throat. "You smell like a summer garden."

"Mr. Romano—"

"Joe."

"Joe. I—I don't think this is appropriate behavior between a cook and her employer."

He laughed softly, his breath warm against her ear.

"Maybe not. But it's perfect behavior between a man and his fiancée."

Lucinda shut her eyes. "I'm not," she said in a small voice that couldn't possibly be hers. "Not your—"

"You are." His arms slid around her; he linked his fingers at the base of her spine. "That's the deal, remember? You agreed to play the part."

"Exactly. I agreed to play it, not to—"

"Shut up," Joe said gently, and his mouth closed over hers.

She held back. After all, she was prepared for this. For his attempt at seducing her. Hadn't she thought it through, just this morning? Hadn't she told herself this was going to happen?

Of course, she had. So she held back. She told herself the kiss was meaningless. That it was, as he'd already made clear, simply part of a game.

But his mouth was so hot on hers. His teeth so sweetly sharp as they nipped at her bottom lip. His arms so strong, his body so hard...

"Lucy," he whispered, "kiss me back."

And she did.

She heard someone—could it be her?—make a sound that was half sigh, half acquiescent moan. She heard Joe's groaned response. And then she stopped thinking and she opened her mouth to his kiss.

He felt her surrender, and the thrill of it dazzled him. He wanted her now, with a ferocity he knew he'd never quench with a thousand cold showers. He could feel his blood pounding in his veins and he wanted to slow down, slow down, to undress her, to touch her, to watch her eyes as he brought her to the edge and kept her there.

Go slowly, he thought, but he was already pulling her arms free of the sleeves of the jacket. Slowly, he told himself, but his hands were undoing the zipper at the back of her dress.

Slowly, dammit, he almost whispered, but she was moaning his name, twisting in his arms, lifting her face to his…

"Lucy," he whispered.

He slipped his hands inside the dress, cupped her breasts. He heard the catch of her breath as his thumbs moved gently against the raised crests.

"Lucy," he said again, as if her name were the only word he could manage. It *was* the only word he could manage. He slid his hands down her spine, under her panties, and cupped her bottom, lifted her into his erection.

"Please," she sobbed, "oh, please. Please, Joe, please…"

There was a sweetness in her desperation. For one timeless moment, as he swallowed her cries, as he caressed her, Joe let himself imagine he was the first, the only lover she'd ever known. The fantasy rocketed through him, blasting its way from the top of his head to his toes.

But that was all it was. A fantasy. And it didn't matter. Nothing mattered but what he was feeling, what he was making her feel.

He kissed her again, his tongue delving deep into the sweetness of her mouth as his fingers slid into the sweetness of her body. Instantly, she cried out; her head fell back and he watched her as she rode the crest of the wave.

He needed her, now. Right now, and he swept her up into his arms.

"Hold on to me," he said roughly, and she pressed her face to his chest, her open mouth against his sweat-soaked shirt, her teeth nipping lightly at his skin as he carried her up the stairs, towards the moment he'd hungered for ever since she'd come into his life, the moment when he was deep inside her and her legs were locked around him.

Somewhere in the distance, a bell rang. Had been ringing, he realized, for a while.

Lucy stiffened in his arms. "Joe?"

"It's the doorbell," he said, and kissed her. "It's all right. We won't ans—"

The front door swung open, hit the wall with a bang. Joe swung around, Lucy still in his arms, and looked down the steps. He saw a clutch of mylar balloons that said Happy Birthday and Congratulations, a huge bouquet of flowers and a magnum of champagne—and two shocked faces, staring back.

"Surprise," his brother said, and grinned.

"Surprise," his sister-in-law said, and blushed.

"Oh, hell," Joe said, and groaned.

The only one who shrieked was Lucy.

CHAPTER NINE

THE little group froze, Matthew and his wife at the door, Joe and Lucy on the steps.

No one spoke.

No one even took a breath.

Everyone waited.

Joe was still holding Lucy in his arms. He knew this moment would be engraved on the interior of his skull forever. His brother, with a grin starting to tilt at his mouth. His sister-in-law, her cheeks turning crimson.

And Lucy in his arms, her heart galloping.

She was going to bolt like a frightened rabbit. He knew it. And he couldn't blame her. If the stairwell suddenly decided to swallow him whole, he'd have died happy.

But that wasn't about to happen, and running away wasn't the answer. It would only make things worse—he could see the devilment growing in Matt's eyes.

Joe put his mouth against Lucy's ear.

"Easy," he murmured.

Easy? Lucy thought in disbelief. She was wrapped around the hated Joe Romano like a vine around a fence post. And he was telling her to take it easy?

Lucy pushed against his chest.

"Put me down."

"I will. Just let me handle this, okay?"

His voice was low. She knew only she could hear it, that the goggle-eyed man and woman standing just inside the door probably thought he was whispering words meant to soothe her. But the look in Joe's eyes was anything but soothing. It was a cold warning, telling her that he was in charge here.

"Put me down, Romano," Lucy said again.

A muscle knotted in his jaw but he did as she'd asked, setting her on her feet, wrapping his hand around her wrist so that his fingers felt like a steel bracelet. He stepped in front of her and she thought, for one wild moment, how wonderful it would be if the action were really protective. It wasn't, of course; she knew that. He was just making sure she didn't say, or do, anything.

He had nothing to worry about. She couldn't think of anything that wouldn't make things worse than they already were. All she could do was hope that this wouldn't take too long, that she'd be able to go to her room, straighten her clothes and get out of this madhouse as fast as possible.

"We seem to have guests," Joe said. "Lucy, this is my brother, Matthew."

Matthew Romano grinned up at them. "Nice to meet you."

"And his wife, Susannah."

Susannah's blush deepened. "Hi."

Lucy searched frantically for an appropriate response. Her mother had spent years drumming what she'd called "deportment" into her head. She knew what to say to a grieving widow, to an elderly maiden aunt, to an unwanted suitor, but what on earth did you say to a pair of strangers who'd caught you—who'd caught you...

"Hello," she said faintly. It seemed to be the right choice. Matthew Romano's grin widened, and the bright color in his wife's face seemed to lessen the slightest bit.

"I thought you two were in New York," Joe said.

"We were." Matt slipped his arm around his wife's waist. "But we got a call from the magazine." He looked at Lucy. "My wife's newest endeavor. It's gonna be terrific, if we can get all the distribution kinks ironed out."

"I don't think Lucy's interested in our problems with *TEMPO* right now," Susannah said, so pleasantly that it almost looked as if the elbow she dug into her husband's ribs was accidental. "We're—we're so sorry about this. We had no idea..."

"We rang the bell. Several times, in fact. " This time, Matthew's grin was downright wicked. "I can't imagine why you didn't hear it."

Susannah shot him an icy look. "I told Matthew not to barge right in, but—"

"But the door wasn't locked. So, here we are."

"Yes," Joe said, "here you are."

"Well." Susannah cleared her throat. "Look, we can come back later, when you, uh, when you and, uh, and—"

"Lucy. My, ah, my new cook."

Matthew's eyebrows shot towards his hairline. "That's not the way we hear it, pal."

Joe felt his heart plummet towards his feet. "You spoke with Nonna?"

"Uh-huh." Matt tugged on the string of one of the balloons. "That's how we heard that congratulations were in order."

"Yes," Susannah said brightly. "What lovely news, Lucy."

"News?" Lucy parroted.

"About you and Joe being engaged. It must have been very sudden."

"Very," Joe said. His fingers tightened around Lucy's wrist. "Isn't that right, honey?"

"No," Lucy said, "no, it—"

"She's right. It wasn't all that sudden." Joe cleared his throat. "I mean, it seems that way but, ah, but we knew, the minute we met, how it was between us."

"Oh," Susannah said, and sighed, "that's so romantic. Matthew? Do you remember when we fell in love? That weekend in Paris—"

"We fell in lust in Paris," Matthew said, but his heart was there, for all the world to see, in the smile he gave his wife.

"He's such a tease," Susannah said gently, and smiled, as well. "What I meant is, it's amazing, how quickly these things can happen."

"Lust?" Matthew said politely.

"Love," his wife replied, ignoring him. "Just look at you two. Strangers, a couple of day ago, and now you're engaged to be married!"

"That's just the point," Lucy said quickly. "We're not—"

"It's okay, honey." Joe's fingers tightened in warning again. "Now that Nonna's let the cat out of the bag, we might as well admit it.'' He gave Lucy a quick look. She'd managed to tug down her dress and close her jacket. The buttons were in the wrong holes, but who cared? He flashed her a big smile, slid his arm around her shoulders, and drew her down the steps with him. ''It's true. We're engaged.''

Susannah sighed. ''How lovely.''

''How sudden.'' Matthew's teeth glinted in a quick smile. ''You didn't say a word yesterday morning when we spoke.''

''I hadn't popped the question yet.'' Joe said.

''Seems to me you hadn't met, either.''

The brothers looked at each other. ''Your timeline must be wrong,'' Joe finally said.

Matthew raised his eyebrows. ''Must be,'' he said lazily. ''Anyway, once we heard the news, we figured we'd stop by and help you celebrate.''

''I said we should have called,'' Susannah hissed.

''No,'' Joe said with a forced smile, ''not at all. It's great, seeing you guys.''

''Well,'' Susanna said after a pause, ''tell us everything. Where did you meet? And when? Have you set a date for your wedding? We're dying for all the details.''

''There aren't any de—''

''It's too soon for details,'' Joe said before Lucy could finish the sentence. ''That's what she means. Isn't that right, honey?''

Lucy glared at him. ''I meant what I said, Romano. Actually—''

''Actually, we're still debating things.'' Joe pulled Lucy close and kissed her. ''Big wedding, small wedding. Evening or afternoon. That kind of thing, you know?''

Matthew nodded. ''Oh, yeah. I know.''

Susannah looked at her husband. ''I thought you liked our wedding.''

''I did,'' Matthew said quickly. ''Of course, I did.''

''Well, that's not how you sounded.''

''But that's what I meant,'' Matthew replied even more quickly. ''Listen, why don't we clear out so you two can, uh, can do whatever you were going to do. I mean, uh, what about having dinner together?''

"No," Lucy said.

"Great," Joe said. "Tonight. The club. Drinks at seven?"

"Seven's fine." Matthew drew his wife closer. "Okay, sweetheart?"

"You told me you liked all the plans I made for our wedding, Matthew. You said—"

Matthew rolled his eyes, turned Susannah towards the door. "See you later," he called over his shoulder.

"Later," Joe said cheerfully.

The door swung shut.

Joe let go of Lucy, hurried to the door, locked it, leaned back against it and blew out his breath.

"Hot damn," he said, and shut his eyes.

"Hot damn, is right. How *could* you, Romano?"

Joe swung around and looked at Lucy. Her jacket was still buttoned wrong, her hair was hanging in her eyes, her cheeks were pink and her mouth was softly swollen. She looked like a woman who'd been doing exactly what she *had* been doing before they were interrupted—but her words rang with indignation.

"I beg your pardon?"

"I said, how could you? Lie that way, I mean. To your brother. To his wife. Letting them think we're engaged…" She took a deep breath and slapped her hands on her hips. "How *could* you?"

"What would you have preferred I tell them?"

"The truth, of course."

"The truth," Joe said coolly. He stuck his hands in his pockets. "Sure. Why not? I should have said, well, we met yesterday. Or you might say we met Friday night. We didn't like each other terribly much, but yeah, we couldn't keep our hands off each other." His mouth twisted. "Is that the 'truth' you wanted me to drop on my brother and his wife?"

Her color deepened. Did he have to put it so bluntly?

"Everything is accurate except the last part." Her eyes flashed. "But that last part is incorrect. I'm not the one's having a problem with my hands, Romano."

Joe thought about pointing out that it was *she* who'd been

begging *him* to take her when Matt and Susannah had come bursting in, but why bother? She was back to being a Boston Ice Queen.

Which was the real Lucinda Barry? Was she the world's greatest actress, or could she turn on and off as fast as a light bulb?

Not that it mattered. Thanks to his brother's unscheduled appearance, Joe could damned near feel his hormones scuttling back into place.

Sex was great—but sanity was better.

A man could always find a woman to bed, but finding your mind after you lost it was a different matter entirely. And he'd definitely gone 'round the bend there, 'round several bends, or so it would seem, coming on to Lucy with all the subtlety of a moose on the loose.

He wasn't blameless, but the fault was mostly hers.

Even dressed in that wacky cook's outfit, she was a woman who could drive a man crazy. Surprise, surprise, he thought grimly. Hell, that was her profession. It was her specialty. She drove men nuts, for a living.

That was why he'd lost control, because she was good at what she did.

Damned good.

Wanting her was axiomatic. It had nothing to do with the soft, warm feel of her in his arms. With her tasting like milk and honey against his tongue. With the way she trembled when he touched her, and whispered his name, as if no man had ever made her feel these things before...

Hell, Joe thought, and scowled darkly.

"Go upstairs, fix your hair, change your clothes."

"I beg your pardon?"

"I said—"

"I heard what you said, Romano. What makes you think you can keep giving me orders?"

Joe looked her up and down. His eyes met hers.

"The fact that I'm the man who has to be seen with you at my club tonight," he said politely. "Any other questions?"

"You've got to be joking! If you really think I'm going to play this game—"

"I don't think it, Blondie, I know it."

Lucy flushed. "I told you not to call me that!"

"And I told you to get out of that ridiculous get-up!"

"No." She folded her arms, angled her chin upward. "This has gone far enough. I should never have agreed to help you torment your poor, sweet old grandmother."

Joe laughed. Lucy gritted her teeth.

"My poor, sweet old grandmother, huh?"

"Yes."

"I don't recall twisting your arm to get you to go along with me."

"Never mind that. You had the chance to tell your brother the truth, and you didn't."

"What'd you want me to do? Was I supposed to say, 'Hey, Matt. Hey, Suze. You know what? The whole thing's a gag.'"

Lucy shrugged her shoulders. "Something like that."

"And what we were doing when they walked in?" Joe snorted with derision. "That was some gag, all right."

"If you're trying to make me think you're gallant, Romano, you're wasting your time."

Joe ran his fingers through his hair. "I just don't see a reason to involve anyone else in this."

"That's because you know it's wrong. It's an ugly deception."

"Oh, I love it! The lady says this is an ugly deception, as if she had no part in setting it up."

"I admit, I went along with the plan, but—"

Joe stalked forward, lowered his head until they were nose to nose.

"But nothing. You're in this, right up to your eyeballs."

"Well, I want out. I hate lying!"

"We're not lying. We're simply assuming a different interpretation of the facts. Thinking outside the box, as it were."

"A charming distinction, if ever I heard one."

"I'm glad you think so, since you're being well-paid to help with the interpretation."

Lucy glared at him. Then she swung away and threw her arms wide.

"I wish I'd told you what I thought of you and your idea, right from the start!"

"Well, you didn't." Joe glanced at his watch. "And we'd better get a move on. Upstairs, out of that silly outfit, into some real clothes. One of those Plain Jane skirts. A shapeless blouse. Another pair of sensible shoes."

"There's nothing wrong with my shoes," she said furiously. "Or with my skirts."

"And comb your hair," he said calmly. "Try leaving it loose."

"Dammit, Romano—"

"Meanwhile, I'll shower and change. We can grab breakfast on the way."

Lucy stamped her foot. "Stop giving orders. On the way to where?"

Joe hesitated. He thought about telling her the truth, that he was taking her downtown to buy something for her to wear tonight, that he was going to stop at a trendy hair salon where he'd once stopped in to pick up a redheaded lawyer he'd been dating, and throw himself—and Lucy—on the mercy of the stylists.

Then he thought about her probable reaction.

"It's a surprise." He saw the surge of color in her face, knew her temper was at the boiling point. "Go on up," he said gently as he clasped her shoulders. "Get out of that silly outfit. Do it, right now, or I'll do it for you."

Lucy's mouth opened, then shut. Her eyes narrowed. He waited for her to tell him what a rat he was, what a no-account, no-good...

"I'll get even with you for this," she said between her teeth.

Then she slapped his hands from her shoulders, turned on her heel, and ran up the stairs.

She came down fifteen minutes later, looking, he decided, like a nun who'd left the cloister.

"Charming," he said politely, taking in her pinned-back

hair, her starched, white cotton blouse, her gray skirt and flat-heeled black shoes.

"I'm so glad you approve," she said, flashing him a smile a barracuda would have envied.

Joe sighed, took her arm, and hustled her through the house, into the garage and into his car.

"Where are we going?"

"We're going clothes shopping," he said as the garage door slid open. "And before you tell me you don't need clothes, just get it through your head that there's no way in hell I'm taking you to dinner with my brother and his wife with you looking like the last girl to be asked to dance at the senior prom."

Lucy flushed. "I suppose you think you look perfect."

"I will, tonight."

He looked perfect now, she thought, glancing over at him. His dark hair was wet from the shower, curling slightly around his ears. He'd put on a gray T-shirt that outlined every muscle of his torso, and faded jeans that looked soft as silk with age.

Heat rolled through her. She thought of how that gorgeous body of his had felt against hers. Of how hot his mouth had been. Of what might have—would have—happened, if his brother and sister-in-law hadn't interrupted them...

"This," Joe said, flooring the gas pedal, "is the last Sunday of the month."

"What a brilliant deduction."

"The club goes in for formal bashes on the last Sunday of every month. That means tuxes for the men, gowns for—"

Lucy sniffed. "I know what it means."

"And?"

"And what?"

"And, do you have a formal gown in your luggage?"

"I'm not going to dignify that with a response."

"Meaning, you don't."

"Meaning, I don't need one."

"No. No, you don't." Joe shot her a tight-jawed look. "You've always got your G-string, for formal occasions."

"I'm not going to dignify that with a response, either."

"You don't have to." The tires squealed as he shot around a corner. "Which is why we're going shopping. You need a dress, shoes, the works."

"If you think I'm going to spend money I don't have, just to soothe your ego—"

"You're right. It's my ego, and my money. Consider what we buy a perk of the job."

"I don't want any perks!"

The tires squealed again as he pulled to the curb. "See, that's the thing about perks, Blondie. You don't have to ask for them. They're part of the package."

"I quit!"

"Too late. We made a deal, remember?"

"It didn't include you buying me clothing."

"How about me buying you breakfast." Joe slammed his door, came around to her side of the car and reached for the handle. "Is that permissible, or am I going to have to get a court order for a feeding tube?"

Lucy glared up at him. Oh, he was so sure of himself. So smug. So damned opinionated...

So spectacularly handsome, she thought, and her heart did that same stupid thing it had done before, turned over behind her ribs so that she felt dizzy.

"Well?" he said.

"I hate you," she muttered.

Joe rolled his eyes, Lucy stepped from the car.

Round two had begun.

At six-thirty, Joe had all but worn a path across the carpet that led from the living room to the library.

He paused at the foot of the steps each time, and looked up. Lucy's door remained firmly shut.

What in hell was taking her so long?

He'd never understood why women took so long to dress. In this case, he understood it even less.

They'd bought only one dress, one pair of shoes, one tiny purse, so she couldn't be doing the female thing, standing in front of her closet in her underwear, trying to decide what outfit to put on.

Joe's footsteps faltered. Dammit, he didn't want to think about Lucy in her underwear.

"Madam will need the proper undergarments," the smiling salesclerk at Neiman-Marcus had said after Joe had finally given the nod to a gown.

"Madam will choose those herself," Lucy had replied, with a look so icy that neither Joe nor the clerk had been foolish enough to argue.

The clerk had brought her a selection of lacy things. Lucy's cold stare had dared Joe to try and see them. He'd wanted to, just to make sure she bought the right things, of course.

Joe stopped pacing, shut his eyes and smiled.

At least he'd seen her in all the dresses. Damned if she hadn't looked magnificent in each and every one. Angry as a cat who'd had its fur stroked the wrong way, sure, but magnificent. That lovely face. The lush body and the long, endless legs, all set off to perfection in gown after gown after gown. All that golden hair, streaming down her back...

The stylist had let it down, oohed, aahed, taken up his scissors and done little more than take off snippets here and there.

Which dress had they ended up buying? He couldn't remember. He'd wanted to buy them all, after a while. The black satin. The blue velvet. The red silk.

It wouldn't matter. Lucy would look perfect in any one of them. He wouldn't have to worry about having to make excuses for what was supposed to be his choice in women to Matt, or to any other guys they might see tonight.

"Joe?"

Lucy's voice was almost a whisper. He turned, looked up the stairs...and knew that the opinions of his brother, or anybody else, had nothing to do with what he felt.

The gown—the red silk, after all—was beautiful. The low, square neckline showed off Lucy's elegant bones; the fluid fabric clung to her high, rounded breasts and slender waist like a sweet memory and the short skirt was the perfect foil for her long legs.

But sackcloth would have done as well. The beauty, the perfection that made his heart lurch, wasn't in the dress.

It was in Lucy.

Her lovely face. Her pale gold hair. The wide eyes and parted, trembling lips...

Joe felt his heart expand so fully that he had to struggle to draw a breath.

Lucy laid her hand on the banister. "Am I—is the dress all right?"

He thought of all the things he might say, all he longed to say. In the end, he only smiled and held out his hand. She looked at it, hesitated, then, slowly, she started down the steps to him.

"You're lovely," he said softly when she reached him.

"It's the gown." She cleared her throat as she lifted her eyes to his. "I want you to know that I'll pay you back, Joe. Once I have a job—"

Joe clasped her shoulders and drew her into his arms. Her body was stiff and unyielding, but he heard her little catch of breath as he gathered her against him, felt the swift kick of her heart against his.

Mine, he thought fiercely, and something primal and male burned its way through his blood.

"You have a job," he said. He cupped the back of her head and tilted her face to his. Her hair, like silken rain, tumbled over his hands. "You're my fiancée. The woman I love, and need, and want."

Lucy's eyes searched his. "For tonight," she whispered.

A muscled knotted in Joe's cheek. "For tonight," he said, and then he bent his head and kissed her until she was clinging to him, and trembling in his arms.

CHAPTER TEN

THE evening was rapidly turning into a disaster.

Under other circumstances, Lucy knew it would have been fun.

Susannah Madison Romano, who'd already been the editor in chief of a major magazine and was now in charge of a new one, was the sort of woman she'd always admired.

Susannah was beautiful, and fashionable, and she could hold her own in any discussion. And yet, for all of that, she was feminine and sweet. And her husband adored her.

He adored his brother, Joe, too. Lucy was certain Matthew would have slugged anybody who'd dare to describe his feelings that way, but the love between the two men was obvious and heartwarming.

That very love for Joe made Matthew suspicious of her. She could see it in his smile, hear it in his voice, and who could blame him? She'd come from out of nowhere, as far as he was concerned. There were times, as the evening stretched on, she found herself wanting to turn to him and say, "Look, it's okay, this isn't real. I'm not your brother's fiancée, I'm not even anyone he cares about..."

But that would only make things be worse, because then the lie she and Joe were living would be in the open. And the ugliness of it would be more than she could bear.

Joe had been right about that, at least. There was no reason to involve anyone else in what they were doing.

So she smiled reassuringly each time she caught Matthew looking at her. She laughed at his funny stories, even though she didn't actually hear them. But it was simple enough to take her cue from Susannah and from Joe. When they smiled, she smiled. When they laughed, she laughed...

And wondered who she despised more, herself or Joe.

They were living a lie, a lie made worse by the kiss Joe had forced on her before they'd left his house.

Except, he hadn't forced it on her. She'd wanted his mouth on hers. His hands on her skin. His breath, mingling with her breath. She'd wanted it, wanted him...and what could be uglier than that, because Joe had kissed her for one reason, and only one reason.

He'd done it to make her look like a woman who'd been loved. A woman who was in love...

She wasn't. Of course, she wasn't.

She was a woman in lust, to borrow Matthew's phrase. And Joe, damn him, knew it.

He hadn't said it, but saying it wasn't necessary when his every action showed it. They were in a public place—a yacht club overlooking San Francisco Bay—and he hadn't touched her improperly, or said much of anything to her. He certainly hadn't kissed her again.

He didn't have to.

She was painfully, agonizingly aware of him, seated beside her.

She tried not to think about him, or about the kiss. Concentrate on your surroundings, she told herself. On the club.

It was a beautiful place. Teakwood floors. Glittering chandeliers. Lovely women and handsome men...

But none as handsome as Joe. None as virile, as rugged, as out and out gorgeously male.

"...sail, Lucy?"

She blinked, looked up. Matthew was smiling across the table at her, his eyes still cool and questioning.

"I'm sorry, Matthew. What did you say?"

"I said, do you sail?"

She nodded. "A little."

"Ah. A lady who can tell a line from a rope," he said, and smiled again, but she knew the simple words were a test.

"Definitely. Some old salts might toss you overboard if you call a line a rope," she said lightly, and smiled back at him.

"So, where did you learn to sail?"

"Back home. On Cape Cod."

"You're from New England?"

She nodded. "Boston."

"Well, that's interesting." Matthew took his wife's hand in his. "Susannah's from that part of the country, too."

"Really," Lucy said politely.

"You two might know some of the same people."

"It's possible."

"Suze?" Matthew said, and looked at his wife.

"New England's a big place," Joe said abruptly. "I doubt if Susannah and Lucy moved in the same circles." He looked at Lucy. "Isn't that right, honey?"

She knew exactly what he meant. Susannah would hardly be likely to know anyone who was friends with a woman who took off her clothes for a living.

Lucy's throat tightened. She wanted to tell him that no matter what he thought, she wasn't that kind of woman, that she'd damned near been raised in clubs as elegant as this one, but what was the point? Let Joe Romano believe what he liked. It wouldn't matter, after tonight. No matter what he said, or did, she was finished with this charade.

Tomorrow morning, bright and early, she was leaving him. She had enough money to get her to the bus station. Once she was there, she'd buy a ticket with whatever she had left. A ticket to anyplace...

"Lucy?"

She blinked. Susannah was looking at her, a gentle smile on her face and a worried look in her eyes.

"Lucy, are you all right?"

"Fine," Lucy said brightly. "I was just—I was thinking about what Joe said and I'm afraid he's probably right. I doubt if we moved in the same circles."

"Well, we can talk about it another time. Over coffee, some afternoon, so we can get to know one another, hmm?"

"Fine," Lucy said again, and hated herself for yet one more lie.

But no lie was as agonizing as the one she kept telling herself, that she hated Joe. That she didn't feel anything for him. That he wasn't the most wonderful man she'd ever met...

She shot to her feet. Three startled faces looked up at her. "I—I'm just going to the ladies' room."

Susannah rose, too. "Great idea," she said briskly.

"Women." Matthew grumbled as he and Joe pushed back their chairs. "The only creatures on the face of the planet who go to the bathroom in packs."

"We do it so we can talk about you," Susannah said fondly.

But they didn't talk about the men. They didn't talk about anything, not until they were both washing their hands at the marble sinks.

"This must be hard for you," Susannah said softly. "Pretending, I mean."

Lucy looked up and met her eyes in the mirror. "I don't know what you're talking about."

"I'm talking about you, making believe you're having a good time, despite my husband's none-too-subtle interrogation techniques." She smiled as she dried her hands on a towel. "Forgive him, won't you? Matthew loves Joe a lot. He's just surprised everything's happened so quickly, that's all."

Lucy saw the color rise in her cheeks. She looked away from the mirror and reached for a towel.

"There's nothing to forgive."

"It's good of you to say that, Lucy. They're just, well, very protective of each other. I suppose it has something to do with the fact that their mother died when they were only kids."

"Did she?"

"Yes. Didn't Joe tell you?"

Lucy shrugged her shoulders. "We haven't had much of a chance to talk about the past."

"Ah." Susannah smiled. "Of course not. You two fell in love so fast. But you have years ahead of you, to learn all about each other."

"Years," Lucy said brightly, and burst into tears.

"Oh, Lucy!" Horrified, Susannah rushed towards Lucy and threw an arm around her shoulders. "Lucy, what is it? What did I say?"

"Nothing. You didn't say... It's just that—that things aren't the way they seem. Joe and I—Joe and I are—"

"Joe's crazy about you."

Lucy looked up, laughed, and reached for a tissue from a box on the marble sink.

"He's not."

"He is. I can see it, each time he looks at you."

"Susannah—"

"And you're crazy about him."

"I'm not." Lucy blew her nose, then tossed the tissue into the basket. "I'm not crazy about him at all. Look, I can't explain, but we aren't—I mean, things between us aren't—"

"You're nuts about my brother-in-law," Susannah said softly.

The women's eyes met in the mirror again, and Lucy knew she was fresh out of lies.

"If I am," she said, her voice trembling, "I'm going to regret it."

She left the ladies' room quickly, before Susannah could respond, and made her way back to the table.

But something had gone wrong there, too. Joe and his brother were silent, not looking at each other. People at the other tables were looking, though, quick little covert glances from behind their wine glasses and champagne flutes.

"Is something wrong?" Susannah finally asked.

"No," both men growled.

Susannah nodded. "Just checking," she said pleasantly.

Silence fell over the table. Something was wrong, all right. Lucy could almost see the hostility in the air. Matthew looked furious, and Joe—Joe looked even worse. His face was all sharp planes and angles, his mouth a thin, hard line.

"Well," Susannah said after a minute, "Joe? Has Lucy seen your boat?"

"No." He said it with finality but that didn't stop Susannah, whose brows lifted.

"You mean, he hasn't taken you for a grand tour of *Lorelei* yet, and shown you what a beauty she is?" She grinned. "And if that isn't enough, Matthew gets to retaliate by asking you to board *Enchantress* so he can tell you the very same thing."

Nobody spoke. Lucy looked at Matthew. His eyes were shuttered, his mouth tight. She looked at Joe. A muscle twitched, high in his cheek.

"The Romano brothers surely love their sailboats," Susannah said with artificial good cheer. "Don't you, guys?"

Still, no one spoke. Lucy looked at Susannah and loved her for trying so hard to overcome whatever had happened in their absence. Susannah looked at her. Say something, her eyes pleaded.

Lucy cleared her throat. "Well," she said into the silence, "what's the difference between the two? Between *Enchantress* and—what was it? The *Laurel?*"

She gasped as Joe grabbed her hand. "Her name is *Lorelei*," he snarled. "*Lorelei*. Is that so difficult to remember?"

"No," Lucy said in surprise, "not really. I simply—"

"There's nothing simple about you, babe. Nothing at all."

His hand clamped around her wrist; she winced as he shot to his feet and all but dragged her up with him. Dimly, she was aware of conversation stopping at the tables around them, of Matthew half rising from his seat, of Susannah stilling him with a touch of her hand.

"Let go of me," Lucy said. "Joe, dammit—"

"That's what she's best at," Joe said, glaring at his brother. "You wanted to know who she was, where she comes from, what she does? Well, this is what she does. She argues. She gives me orders."

"Romano, you—you loud-mouthed brute—"

"She calls me names and drives me crazy." Joe leaned forward and banged his fist on the table. "That's what she does, damn her, and I'm tired of it!"

"Listen," Matthew said, "Joe, take it easy. Just calm down, okay? Just—"

"I'm frigging tired of it," Joe snarled, and strode off.

It would have been a great exit, but he was still holding Lucy by the wrist. And he was taking huge steps, so that she had to run to keep up with him.

"Stop it," she hissed as he hurried her through the dining room. She tried not to look at the faces that turned to watch their passage, all those stares and wide eyes. "Romano, for heaven's sake—"

"Heaven has nothing to do with this," he said as she stumbled after him.

She was right, though. People were staring, and that only made his temper run hotter.

"What are you looking at?" he demanded of a man at a table as they rushed past.

"Why, nothing," the man stammered, "nothing at all."

But Joe wasn't listening. He wasn't thinking, either; somewhere, deep inside his brain, where a semblance of sanity still remained, he knew that. His thought process had been skewed all to hell, and it was Lucy's fault.

It was her fault because she was supposed to act like his fiancée, but she hadn't. That was why Matthew had started asking all those damned questions. Because Lucy hadn't kept her end of the deal. She'd blown it. She hadn't sat close to him, hadn't smiled into his eyes, hadn't touched his hand or laughed at his jokes...

Not that he'd told any jokes, he thought grimly as he shoved open the glass doors that led out onto the dock. Hell, how could a man tell so much as a one-liner when the woman seated beside him wasn't doing her part? Wasn't pretending to belong to him? Wasn't melting against him, the way she had when he'd kissed her at the foot of the stairs tonight. Wasn't sighing his name, touching his face, trembling in his arms?

Oh, yeah. Matthew had caught on, thanks to Lucy.

"What's the deal here, man?" he'd said the minute the women had gone to the powder room.

"What deal?" Joe had replied, looking his brother straight in the eye.

"Don't try and con me," Matt had said sharply. "You're no more engaged to that woman than I am. Who is she, and what's going on?"

So Joe had told him, or he'd tried to. He'd explained about Nonna, and about her matchmaking, and Matthew had listened, and nodded; he'd even laughed when Joe explained the plan, that he'd pretend he was involved with Lucy in order to teach Nonna a lesson.

Except, then, Matt had said, well, the plan would backfire, that Nonna would come to accept his having a fiancée who couldn't cook and wasn't Italian and what would Joe do then?

And Joe, who'd spent the evening watching Lucy act as if she didn't want him, felt the swift, sudden kick of anger in his gut and demanded to know what in hell business that was of Matthew's.

Matt's face had gone white and he'd said, "It's my business because you're my brother. And it looks to me as if this babe has you buffaloed."

And Joe, who knew he'd brought on those words, who'd thought them a zillion times himself, had gone nuts.

He didn't remember much, just jumping to his feet, reaching across the table, grabbing Matt by his stupid bow tie, and then a couple of waiters had come scurrying over.

And, dammit, it was all Lucy's fault.

Joe spun around, grabbed her by the shoulders. "We had an arrangement," he said.

"You let go of me, Romano."

"You were supposed to make my brother think we were engaged."

"He does think we're engaged, more's the pity."

"Not anymore, he doesn't."

"Good. I'm glad you told him the truth." Lucy struggled and twisted, trying to get free. "They're such nice people, your brother and his wife. How could you lie to them that way?"

"It wasn't a lie, it was an arrangement. And you blew it."

"Don't be ridiculous! I did everything I was supposed to do."

"No way."

"But I'm not doing it, anymore. I want out, Romano. Out! You got that? I want—"

"What? Moonlight and roses? Sweet smiles and a ring on your finger?" Joe's hands tightened on her shoulders. "Couldn't you pretend, just for one night?"

"I did pretend! I wanted to tell them the truth, but I didn't. What more do you want?"

"This," Joe snarled, and he dragged her into his arms and kissed her.

It was an angry kiss. A spiteful kiss...and then Lucy made a soft little sound in her throat, and Joe groaned, and everything changed.

"Lucinda," he whispered.

"Joe," she said softly.

He took her face in his hands and kissed her again, his mouth gentle on hers, and she kissed him back, just as gently, and he groaned again and angled his lips over hers, and the kiss changed, went deeper, deeper, until Joe swung Lucy into his arms.

She looped her arms around his neck. "Where are we going?"

"To my boat." He laughed softly, leaned his forehead against hers. "I'll never make it back to the house."

Lorelei was at a slip only a few feet away. He carried her on board, across a teak deck painted ivory by moonlight, and down into the soft darkness of the cabin.

Slowly, he let her slide down the length of his body to her feet.

"Wait," he said softly.

Lucy waited, standing alone in the blackness, trembling with anticipation. Seconds later, moonlight streamed into the cabin.

Joe came back to her and took her in his arms.

"I've done the wrong thing," he said, "all night."

"No. No, it was me. I—I kept thinking how wrong it was, for us to pretend—"

He slid his hands into her hair, stopped her words with a kiss. "I acted as if you weren't there, when all the time I wanted to take you in my arms, kiss you the way I'd kissed you before."

She smiled into his eyes. "Did you?"

"Listen."

Lucy listened. Faintly, like a whisper borne on the breeze, music drifted over the water.

"The band is playing. If we'd stayed in the clubhouse, I'd be asking you to dance just about now." Joe brushed his mouth over hers. "Will you? Dance with me, Lucinda?"

Her throat constricted. This was dangerous. Oh, so terribly dangerous. Something was happening here, something that wasn't supposed to happen...

"Lucy?"

She blinked her eyes, saw Joe step back through a shimmering blur of tears. He smiled, held out his arms, and she sighed and went into them.

He gathered her close, cupped her head, brought it to his shoulder. Oh, he felt so good. Smelled so good. She'd thought about it all evening, how beautiful he was, how gorgeously, flagrantly male in his dinner jacket, so white against his tan and his black-as-midnight hair.

Joe linked his hands at the base of her spine. They were barely moving. Only their bodies swayed in time to the music, in time to the pulsing beat of their blood.

She'd never danced this way before, never wanted to dance this way before. It wasn't the way six-year-old boys and girls were taught to dance, at the Eden School of Dance and Deportment.

"Place your left hand on your partner's shoulder, young ladies," Miss Eden would say briskly over the head of whatever unhappy boy she'd singled out that day. "Now place your right palm against his left palm. No entwined fingers, mind. Backs straight, heads high. Maintain the proper distance between you. Now smile politely and *one,* two, three, *one,* two, three..."

Oh, but this way was so much better.

Joe's breath whispered against her hair. His thighs grazed hers. His chest was hard against the softness of her breasts, and the scent of him rose to her nostrils.

Lucy's breathing fluttered. She could feel the unmistakable hardness of his arousal against her belly and suddenly she was afraid. Not of Joe. Never of Joe. Not of what would happen next, if she let it.

She was afraid of what she felt, of the slowly dawning truth in her heart...

Joe buried his face in her hair. "You're beautiful," he said softly.

"It's—it's the dress."

"It's the woman in it," he said, and pressed his mouth to her throat.

"No," she said quickly, and she drew back in his arms. "Joe..."

He kissed her, his mouth crushing hers, and she knew, she knew. Oh God, she knew.

She'd fallen in love with Joe Romano.

She had to be crazy. Nobody fell in love so quickly. It wasn't possible. It wasn't proper...

With a little sob, she rose to him, opened her mouth to his, and wound her arms around his neck.

Moonlight streamed through the windows, touched her as gently as he was touching her with his hands. And yet, for all his gentleness, she could feel the desire to take her surging within him.

That she had done this to him made her blood drum even faster.

He undressed her slowly, and she knew it was costing him dearly. She could hear it in the raggedness of his breathing, feel it in the occasional roughness of his hands.

Her gown fell away from her like the petals from a rose. She trembled as he looked at her; she had on high-heeled black sandals, and the black lace teddy and sheer black stockings the saleswoman had insisted were the only possible things to wear under the red silk.

"Guaranteed to drive men crazy," the woman had said in a conspiratorial whisper. Lucy, angry and sullen and convinced she would forever hate Joe Romano with all her heart, had said, with cold assurance, that this teddy would *never* drive a man crazy.

How wrong she'd been.

One look at Joe and she knew he was at that point, or maybe

past it. A rush of hunger for him and fear of things she'd only imagined sizzled through her blood at what she saw in his face.

He reached up, jerked his tie open, shrugged off his jacket and let it fall to the floor.

"You are so lovely, sweetheart," he whispered. "So perfect."

Eyes locked to hers, he swept his hands up her body, molding her hips, her waist. She gasped when he cupped her breasts, moaned when he lifted them free of the lacy cups, brushed his thumbs over the crests until they hardened.

"Joe," she whispered. She swayed unsteadily. "Joe," she said again, and he kissed her, his mouth hot and open, and moved his thumbs over her flesh again.

"Undo my shirt," he said roughly.

She did, though it wasn't easy. Her fingers stumbled over the long line of jet-and-gold studs. One after another, they fell to the carpet like scattered drops of rain.

"Now touch me."

Touch him. Oh, yes. Touch him. Touch those hard pectoral muscles. The dark, silky hair that swirled lightly across his skin and arrowed down towards his navel.

Lucy flattened her hands against Joe's chest. The breath hissed from his lungs; he covered her hands with his and held her palms still. He bent his head and kissed her mouth, slowly, then with a growing hunger, tasting her, opening her, teaching her what he wanted and needed.

At last, he drew back and knelt before her. Slowly, he slipped off her sandals, slipped the wispy stockings down her legs, taking time to lift each foot in turn to his lips, to kiss her instep, her arch.

He rose to his feet and stripped away the teddy.

Naked, Lucy stood before him, trembling, fighting back the sudden desire to shield herself from his eyes. No man had ever seen her like this. Joe would never believe that, she thought suddenly, and a sharp pain pierced her heart. But the pain fled, chased by the feel of his lips on hers, by the stroke of his tongue as it sought the warmth of her mouth.

"Beautiful," Joe said softly. "My beautiful, beautiful Lucinda."

He clasped her face in his hands and kissed her again and again. She clasped his wrists, moved closer, moved against him, desperate to feel the thudding beat of his heart.

Joe bent his head. She gasped as he kissed her throat, the slope of her breast, cried out when his lips closed around the yearning tip.

"Joe. Oh, Joe…"

She dug her hands into his shoulders. It was too much. This, the feel of his mouth at her nipple; the stroke of his hand along her hip, down her belly, and then, finally, the touch of it between her thighs…

"Too much," she whispered, "Joe, I can't… I can't…"

He lifted her in his arms, carried her to the bed, placed her in the center of it. Through half-closed eyes, she watched as he stripped off the rest of his clothing. He was even more beautiful than she'd believed, all lean, hard muscle and broad shoulders; his arousal powerful and exciting.

Still, when he came down on the bed beside her, a little rush of fear jolted through her veins.

"Joe. Joe, I've never… I don't…"

"Shhh," he murmured, and took her in his arms, kissed her again and again, until her lips were softly swollen as they clung to his.

"Such a lovely mouth," he said softly, and kissed it. "Such lovely breasts," he said, and kissed them. "Such a lovely belly…"

A cry broke from her throat as he nuzzled her thighs apart.

"No. " She reached down, dug her fingers into his hair. "Joe, you can't…"

Lucy arched like a bow as his mouth found her. The hands that had tried to fend him off seconds ago held him to her; she cried out again as the pleasure of his intimate kiss arrowed through her, racing from his mouth to her breasts, to her very soul.

Light exploded behind her closed eyelids. Nothing had prepared her for this, nothing. And yet, she wanted more. Needed more.

Joe rose above her, entered her on one long, slow thrust.

"Lucinda," he said, "my sweet."

Lucy opened her eyes and looked up at him. "My Joe," she whispered, and lifted her arms to welcome him.

To welcome into her body, her heart and her soul, the man she loved.

CHAPTER ELEVEN

JOE awoke slowly to the gentle rocking of *Lorelei*, the soft patter of rain…

And the warm, sweet-smelling woman lying in the curve of his arm.

It hadn't been a dream. Lucy was here, nestled against him, her golden hair spread over his shoulder. Together, they'd shared a night he knew he'd never forget.

How many times had he made love to her? Through the darkest hours, after the moon had slipped from the sky; in the soft grayness before dawn, and again, just as the new day touched the sky with pink and vermilion, he'd awakened her with kisses, drawn her back against him and come to completion deep inside her.

Just remembering was making him hard as iron. Her soft cries of pleasure, the way she'd clung to him; the catch in her voice when she whispered his name.

And each time, each incredible time, the same ugly thought had been waiting for him as he spiraled back to earth.

How many other men had known her like this? How many would know her in years to come?

Damn all the salesmen in the world to hell.

Joe shut his eyes and took a couple of deep breaths. What was he doing, thinking that way? A woman was entitled to the same sexual freedom as a man. He'd always believed that.

It was just that this woman led a life he didn't understand.

But it was none of his business. None whatsoever.

None, dammit, he thought, and he rolled away from her, rose from the bed and headed for the shower stall that adjoined the cabin.

He dried off, put on a pair of shorts and headed topside. The rain had eased off. Fine. He'd walk to the fast-food place at the end of the dock, buy a couple of containers of coffee. Then he'd wake Lucy, give her time to dress, drive her home and tell her...

Tell her, the deal was off.

Of course.

Joe felt as if somebody had lifted a rock from his chest.

They'd slept together. Fine. Great. Sex was where they'd been heading since they'd first laid eyes on each other. That was what all the sniping had been about, just an edgy little mating dance leading to the Big Moment.

Well, the Big Moment had come and gone. The thing about giving his nonna a scare had come and gone, too. A dumb idea, now that he'd had time to think it through. So, things had worked out just fine. What more could a man ask for? Great sex with a gorgeous babe. A guarantee his grandmother probably wouldn't interfere in his love life without thinking twice about it, at least for a while...

"Hi."

He swung around. Lucy was standing at the top of the ladder. She was wearing a pair of his cut-offs, one of his T-shirts, and her feet were bare. Her hair tumbled in a wild cloud down her back.

She looked, for all the world, like a woman embarrassed to find herself on a man's turf the morning after a wild night spent in his arms.

A fist seemed to close around Joe's heart. Yeah, he thought coldly, right. She was about as embarrassed to find herself facing him in the daylight as the Venus de Milo would be to discover she had no arms.

"Hi," he said briskly. "Sleep well?"

Her color deepened. Well, dammit, why wouldn't it? What a stupid thing to have said. Joe frowned, cleared his throat.

"I mean, some people have trouble adapting to the rocking of a boat."

"Not me." She smiled slightly and lifted her hands to her hair. The action lifted her breasts and he tried not to think about the honeyed taste of them, or their silken feel. "We had a boat when I was growing up. Not a sailboat, like this. A cabin cruiser.''

"In Boston," he said, forcing his eyes from her body to her face.

"Uh-huh. Well, actually, my father kept it out on the Cape, in this little town..."

"Boats are expensive."

"Oh, I know. But my father used to say..." She broke off. Joe was looking at her with such a cold expression in his eyes. "Never mind." She gave a quick laugh. "Why would you want to hear about my father's stinkpot?"

"Yeah." Joe flashed a tight smile in acknowledgment of the little war that had always raged between rag sailors and those who preferred the swiftness of gasoline engines. "Did your family have money?"

Lucy turned away. "I don't really want to talk about—"

"Maybe I do." He caught her arm, swung her towards him. He knew he was holding her too hard, that his hands were bruising her, but hell, there was a bruise inside him, too, one he couldn't figure out. "So, what's the deal, Blondie? Poor little rich girl, tired of living the good life, decides to strike out on her own?"

"Let go of me, Joe!"

"No. No, seriously, I want to hear about it. I grew up poor, you see. Not a penny in my jeans that I didn't earn, from the time I was maybe ten years old until today."

"Good for you," she said tightly. "Now, let go."

"I used to crew on a couple of charter boats, times I wasn't breaking my ass on my old man's fishing boat. And I saw them, the kids who'd grown up rich, the girls who thought it would be fun to get their kicks by rolling around in the mud for a while."

He saw the quick glitter of angry tears rise in her eyes and he told himself to stop, that how she lived, what she did, wasn't his concern.

But it was. She'd spent the night in his arms, awakened in his bed. And even though he knew what she was, he was having trouble imagining spending tonight, any night, without her. He couldn't imagine awakening without her in his arms.

The realization infuriated him.

"Is that what you've been doing, Blondie? Huh? Taking a walk on the wild side, just to get even with life?"

"You bastard."

Her voice was low, tremulous, and she began to weep. Good. Let her cry. He wanted to shake her. Shake her hard, until she admitted that when she was in his arms, he made her feel—he made her feel...

He let go of her, stepped back. "Get your things," he said tonelessly. "I'll drive you home."

"It's not my home, and they're not my things. They're yours. And I don't want them."

She looked up at him. His eyes were almost black; his jaw, shadowed and unshaven, was thrust forward. He looked dangerous and exciting, and the love she felt for him, the hate she felt, were almost more than she could bear.

A choked sound broke from her throat and she put her hand over her mouth and shoved past him.

"Lucy," he said, but she kept on going, off the boat, onto the dock, towards the clubhouse and the parking lot. She heard him give a muffled curse, and then he strode past her, towards the Ferrari.

The rain picked up as they drove back to Pacific Heights. Lucy sat stiffly beside Joe, her eyes focused on the wet road, her hands tightly laced in her lap.

The windshield wipers brushed against the glass.

"Luce-in-dah," they whispered. "Luce-in-dah, what have you done?"

She'd made a mistake, was what she'd done. A terrible mistake.

She should never have let Joe make love to her. Never. Nev—

Let him make love to her? She bit down on her lip to keep from laughing. Or from crying. One or the other, it didn't matter. She hadn't "let" Joe do anything. She'd urged him on, she'd wanted all of it. Everything. Each kiss. Each caress. Each wild, sweet, amazing moment. The feel of him, deep inside her. The ecstasy of his possession.

Okay. She'd done it, and now it was over. All of it. Their ridiculous arrangement was finished. As soon as they reached his place, she'd pack and leave. She'd walk downtown, hitch a ride. Get to the bus terminal, buy a ticket for wherever her money would take her, even if it was only twenty miles up the road.

Goodbye, Joe Romano.

She glanced at him, saw the thin, tight line of his mouth, the white-knuckled grip of his hands on the steering wheel. A sob caught in her throat and she looked quickly away, fixed her eyes to the windshield and the rain and the road.

What was there to cry about, dammit? She was a grown woman, she'd given herself to a man. So what? It wasn't as if she'd been "saving" herself. She didn't have any hang-ups about sex between consenting adults. Oh, yeah, maybe, just maybe, she'd had this silly idea tucked away, about someday finding the right man, someone she'd want to give the gift of her virginity.

God knew, she'd never wanted to give it to the man she'd been engaged to marry.

Lucy huffed out a breath.

Some gift. Some "right man." Some stupid, inane, humiliating thing to have done with a guy who thought she was some little rich girl rebelling against her soft life by sleeping her way through half the male population of the United States of America.

The house was just ahead. Joe hit the remote on the dash; the garage door slid up and he pulled the car inside and killed the engine. Lucy undid her seat belt and reached for the door handle.

"Lucy."

She turned and looked at him, her chin lifted. "Yes?"

"The deal is—"

"—off." She smiled. She hoped she was smiling, anyway. "Indeed it is. And it won't take me five minutes to pack my—"

"I'm not going to pretend," he said roughly. "Not to my brother, or my sister-in-law, or my grandmother. It was a stupid thing to do, from the start."

"I tried to tell you that," she said, and reached for the door handle again. Joe's hands fell on her shoulders and he turned her to face him.

"They can accept the fact that you're my mistress or not. The choice is—"

Lucy blinked. "What?"

"I know I promised to pay you, but things are different now. What I'll do is open a checking account in your name and deposit a sum into it. When you need more, just tell me. I'll arrange for charge cards, too. Saks. Neiman-Marcus. Whatever stores you prefer."

Obviously, he'd lost his mind.

"You've lost your mind," she said.

"Actually, it's an eminently workable solution."

He looked truly sincere. She'd seen that look before, on the faces of TV pitchmen.

"Unfortunately, I can't tell you how long it will last. I mean, I know it's a good deal for both of us, and you'd like to have some sort of timetable, but—"

She didn't even think about it, she just hit him as hard as she could, her fist flying through the air and connecting with his jaw with a satisfying smack. His head jerked back; his eyes crossed. Good, she thought furiously, good, you miserable, no-good, smug, stupid son of a bitch!

Unfortunately, he recovered fast. She was half out of the car when he reached for her.

"Oh, hell," Lucy said, and ran.

"Dammit, Lucinda," Joe roared, and went after her.

The door that led into the house wasn't locked. She breathed a sigh of relief, shoved it open, raced for the stairs.

Joe caught her when she was only inches from the safety of her room. She yelped as he swung her around, shoved her back against the wall, pinned her there, his hands clasped around her wrists.

"Is that all you know how to do? Ball up your fist and let

fly?'' He leaned closer. "Lucinda. You're driving me crazy. What more do you want from me?''

His voice was low and menacing. If he'd looked dangerous before, there were no words for the way he looked now.

Lucy shuddered and tried to break free.

"I don't know what you want," he said. "And you won't tell me.''

"Just let go of me, Romano. I'll be out of this house and your life so fast, it'll make your head spin.''

He shifted his weight so that his body brushed lightly against hers. She could feel the heat emanating from him like waves of tightly banked fury.

"Tell me it was all an act last night, and I'll let go.''

He looked down at her, his gaze like a stroke of flame over her parted lips, and she felt the swift, hot swell of desire low in her belly that only he could satisfy.

Don't be a fool, she told herself, Lucinda Barry, don't be stupid!

"Just tell me you didn't feel what I felt, when we made love." He bent to her and she tried to twist her face away, but he found her mouth with his, kissed her until her lips parted. "Lucy," he whispered, "Lucy, you know that we're not done with each other yet. Tell me what you want, and I'll give it to you.''

Your love, she thought, but she had some pride left, though not enough to keep her from lifting her tear-stained face to his and opening just enough of her heart to let him see some of what was inside.

"I don't want your money. I don't want to be your—your kept woman.''

Joe smiled. It was such an old-fashioned phrase and yet, it sounded so right on her lips.

"Just say you want me," he said gruffly, and released her wrists, and she gave him the only answer she could by thrusting her hands into his hair, drawing his face down to hers, and kissing him.

"You're kidding," Matthew said, and slammed down his bottle of ale hard enough so some of the liquid sloshed onto the glass-topped table on the patio behind his home.

Joe gave a dry laugh. "Do I look as if I'm kidding?"

Matthew looked his brother over cautiously. "No," he admitted, "I guess not." He hesitated, tried to figure out how to phrase the question, then gave up trying. "So, you asked Lucy to, uh, to be your..."

Joe nodded.

"Does Nonna know?"

Joe shook his head again. "She still thinks we're engaged. I keep meaning to tell her, but..."

"Yeah, okay." Matthew drank some ale. "What about the cooking thing? I mean, Lucy was supposed to—"

Joe looked up. "If you'd ever tasted a meal Lucy made, you wouldn't even ask the question."

"Well, who does it, then?"

"Matt, you know, you are some piece of work. I just told you that I've asked a woman to live with me, and all you can think of is your stomach."

"Actually," Matthew said in an aggrieved tone, "I'm thinking of *your* stomach. Eating is another appetite a man has to—" Joe shot him a cold look. "Sorry," Matthew said quickly. "I only meant—"

"I know what you meant. And you're right. That's what she's there for, because she's fantastic in..."

In bed, he wanted to say. But he couldn't. What in hell was wrong with him? Matt and he had always shared stuff. They'd talked about how tough the old man could be when things hadn't gone right for him. About how they missed their mother. And yes, they'd talked about women, the kind of conversation guys had and women despised them for having...

Well, not about all women. Matt had never said anything derogatory or intimate about Susannah, but that was to be expected because she was his wife. He loved her. That was why it was crazy, that he, Joe, couldn't bring himself to talk about Lucy, and what she was like in bed. She wasn't his wife. She wasn't even his mistress. And heaven knew, he didn't—he didn't...

Joe frowned, hoisted his bottle of ale and took a long, cold swallow.

"Actually," he said with what he assumed was an easy smile, "we cook together."

"You cook? Both of you?"

"Uh-huh."

"But you just said—"

"Well, she's learning, the same as I am. She's pretty good at desserts. Coconut cake, chocolate mousse, stuff like that. And she has this collection of cookbooks, see, so what we do is, we pick a recipe. Then she buys the ingredients…"

"With what? You said she's broke, and she won't take any money from you."

"She finally agreed to let me give her a charge card for the supermarket."

"Ah." Matthew nodded as if he understood what his crazy kid brother was talking about. So far, all he knew was that Joe, who'd never even let a woman spend the entire night in his bed, was living with a woman he'd met fourteen days ago. "So, okay. You pick a recipe. She buys the stuff that goes into it."

"Yeah. And then we cook it, together, for supper."

"You cook it, together."

Matt tried not to grin. Apparently, he didn't succeed because Joe shot him a belligerent look.

"What's so funny, Romano? You never heard of a guy learning to cook?"

"No, no. I mean, of course I have. I even like to putter in the kitchen with Susannah."

"So?"

"So, it just sounds so—so domestic."

Joe flushed. "It's survival, is what it is. Hell, my gut can only tolerate just so much take-out fried chicken."

"You never used to mind take-out."

"Yeah, well, a guy needs change."

"Right," Matthew said, and tried to figure out where to take the conversation next. "So, uh, so if Lucy won't accept any money from you, what's she living on?"

Joe's mouth thinned into a narrow line. "What in hell is that supposed to mean?"

"It means what it sounded like, kid. How's she supporting herself? Does she have some kind of talent?"

Joe shot out of his chair, reached across the table, grabbed a handful of Matthew's shirt and dragged him to his feet.

"I don't like what you're suggesting."

"That's the second time you've put your fist in my throat because of this woman. And I don't like it." Matthew's eyes went flat and cold. "Let go, Joe."

The men glared at each other for a few seconds. Then Joe made a choked sound, let go of Matthew's shirt, and stepped away from the table.

"I think I'm losing my mind," he said softly.

Matthew nodded. "That makes it unanimous. What the hell is the matter with you?"

"I don't know."

"Look, maybe you're in over your head. Hormones can do weird things, even to adult men." Matthew walked to his brother's side and slung a comforting arm around his shoulders. "Forget what I said the last time. I've changed my mind. Lucy seems like a nice girl. I'm sure, if you explained things to her, that you made a mistake, asking her to stay—"

"She *is* nice. She's got a terrific sense of humor. She loves to sail. She's got a green thumb—she bought a bunch of plants for that big window in the living room. Well, she didn't actually buy 'em. She saw them, see, by the curb outside somebody's house, waiting for garbage pickup. They were all dying, and she said she felt sorry for them, so she brought them home and now they look great. And I taught her to play pool and now she can beat me. Did I mention that?"

Only two or three dozen times, Matthew thought, and sighed.

"Okay. So she's wonderful. Still—"

"She is. Wonderful, I mean."

"Yeah, but if you feel crowded—"

"I don't. She has this thing. This, uh, this quality, you know? She can be so quiet, I have to look up to make sure she's there. At night, when we sit in the living room and read, or maybe watch TV—"

"You stay home and watch TV?"

"Or read. Or, like I said, play pool..." Joe stared at Matthew. "Holy cow," he groaned, "it really does sound domestic."

"Joe," Matthew said gently, "I think you're in love with Lucy."

"Hell, no!" Joe broke away from his brother's encircling arm. "I'm never going to fall in love. What's the sense? You love a woman, you marry her, and the two of you end up the way Mom and Pop did, her hoping you haven't had a bad day and cringing if you did, you sitting in the corner, wondering how you ever let yourself get into this mess and hating the world..."

"That was Mom and Pop," Matthew said. "It isn't everybody. Look around you, Joe. People can be happy together. Look at Susannah, and at me."

Joe tucked his hands in the back pockets of his trousers.

"Maybe," he said after a pause. He looked up. "But that doesn't mean I'm in love with Lucy." He gave a wry laugh. "Believe me, you wouldn't want that."

"Why not? I just said, she seems nice. Sweet, and caring—"

"She's a stripper, for God's sake!"

Matthew stared at Joe. "A what?"

"You heard me," Joe snarled. "The first time I saw her, she was wearing a handful of spangles and a smile, and she was popping out of a cake at a private party."

Matthew felt behind him for a chair and sank into it. "Oh, hell."

"Exactly." Joe paced the length of the patio, then paced back. "You want me to be in love with a woman like that?"

"No. No, of course not." Matthew stood up. "No way."

"Why not?" Joe's eyes grew dark. "You saying she's not good enough for the Romanos?"

"No," Matthew said cautiously. "But you said—"

"She says it isn't true. That she never even jumped out of a cake before, or entertained at a bachelor party."

"Well," Matthew said even more cautiously, "maybe she's telling you the—"

"She says she comes from this old-line family in Boston. That they were rich."

"Well, okay. Maybe she's—"

"She's got some story about only being at that damned bachelor party because it was catered by a cooking school, and she had to agree to do the cake thing so she could get her diploma, because she went to a boarding school where they never taught her how to make a buck and now she has to support herself." Joe's eyes shot sparks. "You tell me, Matt, would any intelligent man swallow that?"

Matthew shrugged his shoulders. It seemed the only safe thing to do.

"And she says…" Joe's voice fell to a rough whisper. "She says there's never been anybody but me." He looked up, his very posture daring Matthew to argue. "Okay. She doesn't actually say it. But she acts it." Color striped his cheekbones. "When we—when we make love. If you know what I mean."

"I can figure it out," Matthew said quickly, and held up his hands. "Joe, listen. I think you need to have a long talk with the lady. Could be, you've figured her wrong."

The look on his brother's face almost broke Matthew's heart. "You think?"

"Yeah," Matthew said, and cleared his throat, "I think. And I think you need to have a talk with yourself, too." He clapped Joe on the back as they walked slowly along the path that led to the front of the house. "An honest talk, about what you feel for her. You know what I mean?"

Joe nodded. "Maybe she's been telling me the truth," he said quietly. He took a deep breath. "And even if everything I think is true…well, people change. Isn't that right, Matt?"

Matthew thought of his brother as he'd been in his teens, always getting in trouble; he thought of him as he'd been the last few years, working his tail off to make a name for himself in the city's financial world, dating every beautiful woman who came his way but never giving away his heart…

"Yeah." He swallowed hard. "Yeah, bro, they do."

*   *   *

Joe headed home, driving a little more slowly than usual. He had a lot to think about.

He was glad he'd stopped by to see Matt. The visit had been an impulse; it was a quiet Friday, nothing much happening except drinks with a client at five, but the guy had canceled. So Joe had phoned his brother, just to touch bases. One word led to another and they'd agreed it would be cool to leave their respective offices early and meet at Matt's place for a drink.

"What's the sense of being the man in charge, if you can't play hooky once in a while?" Matt had said, and Joe had laughed and said that made sense to him.

He sighed, geared down and stopped at a red light.

The truth was, he'd been wanting to talk with Matthew. So much had been going on in his life lately: Matt wasn't the only one shocked to learn he'd asked a woman to live with him. He was shocked, too, and he'd been the one who'd done the asking.

Of course, it was temporary, until either he or Lucy decided it was time for a change.

Joe frowned.

He knew it would happen. He'd grow bored, or she would. Sure. It was just a matter of time. Why would he think otherwise? Had he lost his perspective?

Maybe so. Maybe that was why he'd wanted to see Matt, who was always clearheaded and logical. Well, not a couple of years ago, when he'd met Susannah. Matt had turned into a man who didn't know which way was up.

Joe's frown deepened. The light turned green and he jammed his foot down on the gas pedal.

Yeah, Matt had done some strange things when he fell for Suze, but so what? If *he* was acting weird, it was only because he wasn't accustomed to living with a woman.

Love didn't have a damn thing to do with it.

No way was he falling for Lucy.

She was good in bed. Okay, so she was good to be with out of bed, too. What did that prove?

"Nothing," Joe muttered. "Not one thing."

Joe pulled the Ferrari into the driveway, shut off the engine.

Dammit, he had to know. Had she really done the things he thought she had? Would he have to look at every guy in the city and wonder if she'd been with him?

It was nuts to think a woman who'd perform at bachelor parties could have possibly hung on to her virginity, but that first night they'd been together had been different from every other night he'd ever spent with a woman.

The nights since, too. Lucy's reactions to the things he did. Her breathless excitement when he touched her. Her intoxicating hesitancy when she explored his body with her hands, her mouth.

Joe held his breath. Was it possible that she hadn't lied? That she'd never danced for a roomful of men, or been with anyone before him?

Was he her first lover? Her first love?

Joe jumped from the car and ran to the house.

"Lucy?" he called as he jammed his key in the lock. "Lucy, honey, we have to talk."

He knew, right away, that she wasn't home. Otherwise she'd already have been at the door and in his arms, the way she was each night as soon as she heard him, her beautiful face turned up for his kiss.

His smile dimmed, but only for a second. Okay, she wasn't here. But she wouldn't have expected him home for another couple of hours. It was only that the place seemed so empty without her.

"Lucy," he said softly, and a thousand different emotions flashed through him, all of them pointing in one direction.

He loved her.

And she was in love with him.

That was why she'd been so furious that morning on the boat. She'd known then that she loved him, but he'd been too dense, too dumb, too all-around selfish to see it.

Joe sank down on the bottom step and ran his hands through his hair.

He was in love.

"Romano," he whispered, "you blind son of a bitch, you've loved her from the beginning."

He grinned, jumped to his feet, ran up the stairs and checked the rooms, just to make sure they were empty. Then he ran down to the kitchen. Lucy was probably out shopping for their dinner. What was it they'd figured for tonight? Shrimp jambalaya, that was it.

Well, forget that. Cooking was fun. Everything was, with Lucy. But when a man poured out his heart, told a woman he loved her and that, okay, he'd been busy making an ass of himself and could she possibly forgive him?—when a man did that, it called for dinner at the best restaurant in the city and chilled Cristal champagne.

He reached for the telephone, punched the speed-dial number for Le Peregrine. "Good afternoon," a smooth-as-velvet voice said, "would you please hold?"

Joe rolled his eyes. "No problem." Then he switched the phone to his left ear, pulled a notepad towards him, picked up a pencil...

What was that, on the notepad? A list of some kind. And a name and address.

The smile died on his lips as his gaze skimmed over the pad.

"Five o'clock," he said softly as he read aloud. "Private party. Swinging doors. Back room. Blue Mountain Café, Charles Street."

Joe knew the place. Knew of it, anyway. It was a small club. Very private. He'd never been there but it had a reputation...

He hung up the phone. The notepad trembled in his hand. The words were hard to decipher. Lucy must have jotted them down in a rush—or was it the sudden clouding of his vision that was making it so difficult to see?

"Bikini." His voice was rough as gravel as he read the list out loud. "Pasties. Pom-poms. Melted chocolate. Whipped cream."

Joe could feel his heart shriveling, turning from warm flesh to cold, hard stone. Carefully, he put down the notepad, walked to the window and stared blindly out at the tiny flower garden in front of the house. A couple of minutes passed. Then he went back, picked up the pad and read the list again.

He wanted to pound his fist through the wall. The desire to hurt something, destroy something, was almost overpowering. Instead, he ripped the page from the pad and stuck it in his pocket.

With a head full of rage and a heart full of anguish, he ran out to his car and roared down the driveway.

A fog was rolling in. He drove by instinct, faster than he should. Horns blared; he caught a quick glimpse of the red, angry face of a cable car operator, got an impolite gesture from a guy in a car he cut off, but nothing mattered except the piece of paper burning a hole in his pocket.

That, and the woman he'd been fool enough to think he loved.

"Damned idiot," he muttered as he pulled to the curb in a no-parking zone outside the Blue Mountain Café.

Love? A woman like Lucinda Barry?

Joe barked out a laugh as he pushed through the doors into the club. New! New! New! a sign shouted. Private Parties, Our Specialty!

"I'll bet," he said, his mouth twisting.

A man came hurrying out from behind a high desk. "May I help you, sir?"

Joe had already spotted the swinging doors that led to the back. He kept walking.

"Sir, you can't go in there. There's a party in progress."

"I know all about your parties," Joe snarled. The guy made a grab for his arm. Joe swatted him aside, slapped his hand against the swinging doors and felt the swift pulse of blood through his veins as he stepped into the room where, even now, Lucy might be standing on a stage in front of a bunch of slobbering, hot-eyed sons of bitches...

And saw, instead, a bunch of helium-filled balloons, a clown with a big red nose and an even redder wig, and tables packed with little kids. Four-year-olds. Five, maybe. He didn't know much about kids.

And Lucy. His Lucy, wearing a long-sleeved, pale pink dress and a pair of her ever-sensible shoes, staring at him from behind what looked like an old-fashioned soda fountain, staring at him as if he were an apparition while she held a bowl of whipped-cream-and-chocolate-covered ice cream in her out-stretched hand.

"Joe?"

He stared back at her while he tried to get his tongue unstuck and his brain into gear.

"Joe?" Lucy said again. She shot him a tentative smile, handed the dish to the kid who reached up for it, and came out from behind the fountain. "What are you doing here?" she asked as she walked towards him. She put her hand on his arm while her smile went from tentative to puzzled.

Joe opened his mouth, closed it again. "I... I... I..."

"Yuck, yuck, yuck," the clown said, and the little kids laughed and clapped their hands.

Lucy blushed, took Joe's arm and led him out through the swinging doors to the club's lobby.

"Joe, for goodness' sake, say something. How did you know I was here?"

In slow motion, like a man trapped in a bad dream, Joe took the piece of notepaper from his pocket.

"I came home early. You weren't there, but this was. "

She frowned, took the paper from him and glanced at it. "Oh, yeah. I forgot it. Good thing I remembered the stuff I needed to pick up, and the address, too."

"You're working a private party," Joe said slowly. "At the Blue Mountain Café."

"Uh-huh." She smiled. "The *new* Blue Mountain Café. Miss Robinson made that very clear."

"Miss Robinson," Joe repeated carefully.

"Yes. Oh, that's right, you never met her. Well, she's wonderful. She was a dancer when she was young. She's an old woman now, but she has more spirit and energy than..." Lucy laughed. "Let me just tell you the news. I called Miss Robinson a few days ago, just to see how she was doing, and she told me she'd bought this place—"

"An old lady bought the Blue Mountain?"

"Yes. Seems it had been closed for a while, that it had an

awful reputation, but she bought it, renovated it, and turned it into a place that caters parties for children.''

"For children," Joe repeated. It seemed all he was capable of doing.

"Exactly. And she asked if I were still working as a chef—for you, she meant.'' A soft blush suffused Lucy's cheeks. ''I said I wasn't, and she said she might have some work for me and that she'd call, if she ever did, and then, this morning, she phoned and said her desserts person had the flu and how was I at making… Joe, what is it?''

"Nobody needs this stuff for desserts," he said gruffly, snatching the list from her. "A bikini. Pasties. Pom-poms. Melted chocolate. Whipped cream.''

"That's 'blini,' not 'bikini.' Well, of course, blini are usually for grown-ups but I thought of filling them with ice cream and…'' Lucy's smile faded. She looked up, her eyes meeting his. "Oh, Joe," she said softly.

Joe cleared his throat. "Well, hell, what was I to think? 'Pasties.'''

"Pastries.''

"And pom-poms.''

"A dessert I remembered from my own childhood. My mother didn't approve, but the cook took pity on me and made them once in a while. Chocolate cupcakes, frosted with white icing, then dusted with coconut…'' Lucy stepped back. "You thought,'' she said, her voice trembling, "you thought I was here, entertaining men.''

Joe looked at her. Her mouth was trembling even more than her words, her eyes were glassy with tears, but it was the look in those eyes, those beautiful eyes, that sent a spear of panic into his heart.

"You thought that of me, Joe. That—that I would lie in your arms at night, and—and during the day, do the kinds of things that went on in the Blue Mountain Café before Miss Robinson bought it.''

"Lucy. Honey, no. I didn't. I just—''

She jumped back as he reached for her. "Don't touch me!''

"Sweetheart. Lucinda, please—''

"I told you not to touch me!" Lucy's face was white, her eyes almost black. "What a fool I was, to let myself fall in love with you."

Her unexpected admission filled him with joy. "That's what I'm trying to tell you," Joe said. "I'm in love with you, too."

"No. You aren't." She jabbed a finger, hard, into the center of his chest. "It's that oversized ego of yours. It's all puffed up because you think I'm this—this cheap version of Salome all men seem to fantasize about."

"No," he said with hot indignation. "Dammit, I never—"

"You came here, expecting to see me leaping out of a cake. Or peeling off my G-string." She jabbed him again. "Isn't that right?"

"Yes. I mean, no. I mean, I thought that might be it. But—"

"You don't love me, Romano. You don't trust me. You don't even like me." Tears rolled down Lucy's face. "I'm just some kind of—of sexual toy to you. A trophy you figured you'd keep around for a while and then dump when things got dull."

Joe blinked. "Lucinda. You're distorting everything."

"I'm not," she said, and suddenly her shoulders sagged and her hands fell to her sides. "I'm not," she said, very softly, and brushed past him.

"Sir," an officious voice said, "I tried to tell you earlier, you cannot—"

Joe snarled, grabbed the clerk by the elbows, lifted him off his feet and set him aside, but it was too late.

Lucy had gone out the door and disappeared into the fog.

CHAPTER TWELVE

JOE stepped into the center of the sidewalk and peered up and down the street.

The fog was getting denser, lending a surrealistic look to things. Swirls of it curled around people hurrying past him. Their faces seemed to float above disembodied torsos and legs.

None of those faces was Lucy's.

Fear twisted his belly with a steely grip. He crushed it down, ruthlessly, with a jolt of anger.

"Dammit," he said under his breath, and cut across the pavement to his car.

She was good at this, Ms. Lucinda-of-the-Boston-Barrys.

Joe jammed the key into the ignition and started the engine. The lady got ticked off at him, she walked out.

Well, she wasn't getting away with it this time, anymore than she did the last. A woman couldn't just march out of a man's life because he said something that annoyed her. When you came down to it, what had he done, anyway, except tell her he was in love with her, and that only went to prove how crazy she'd made him.

He slowed the car to a crawl, ignored the honks of protest from the traffic behind him, and put down the window so he could check out faces he drove past.

Only a masochist would love a woman whose greatest joy, whose special skill, lay in knowing how to drive him up the wall. Lucy was beautiful. Okay. And she was bright. But he'd dated lots of bright, beautiful women, and not a one—

"Not a blessed one," he snarled, slapping his hand against the steering wheel.

Not one of those babes had done a number on his head the way this one had.

Plus, she had a quick temper. She didn't know the meaning

176

of compromise. She didn't seem to know how to stroke a man's ego, or care about doing it.

And that was only the start.

Lucy couldn't cook, not unless you thought desserts constituted "cooking," and not even he, with his cast-iron stomach, could live on chocolate and whipped cream forever.

She probably couldn't sew or knit, either. He'd bet anything she didn't know how to clean a house. She was probably lousy at any of those female things.

Joe stopped at a red light.

Okay, he'd taught her to play a mean game of eight ball. He hadn't had to teach her to argue politics and world affairs; she could talk even him under the table with facts and figures, and that was saying a lot. For all he knew, she could hold her own in a discussion of particle physics.

On top of all that, she had a great sense of humor and a wonderful laugh. She was sweet and good and kind. And yes, she was special, in bed...

Joe blew out his breath.

Okay. More than special. He felt something when they made love, felt it even afterwards, just holding her in his arms, something he'd never felt before.

So what?

Was that enough to make a man tolerate her damn fool stubbornness? He'd told her he loved her, for God's sake. That he'd been wrong, in his judgment of her. What more did she want? Was he supposed to say he wanted her with him, always, that he wanted her to be his wife?

Because he did, dammit.

He did.

His anger fled and the fear came back. He had to find her. Had to make her see that he didn't view her as a trophy, as the star of some juvenile fantasy. He loved her. Needed her. Wanted to share his life with her.

And, by God, if she didn't believe him, if she didn't admit that she felt the same way, he'd toss her over his shoulder and carry her off, the way he'd done before.

The light went from red to green. Joe wrenched the wheel and made a quick, hard, illegal U-turn.

A guy in the next lane shouted something.

"You don't understand, man," Joe yelled, "I'm in love."

The guy rolled his eyes, made a face, and gave Joe a thumbs-up.

"Thanks," Joe said.

Something told him he was going to need it.

Lucy was running down the hilly pavement, one block over.

The fog was getting worse.

Good, she thought grimly. Joe would never find her in this soup, even if he knew where to begin.

And he didn't. She was certain of it.

Right now, he was probably driving that testament-to-testosterone that he called an automobile up and down the street where the café was located, searching for her.

She could picture it, picture him, getting angrier by the second. He'd never calm down long enough to stop and think logically. If he did, he might figure out that she'd run to the corner, watched him leave the Blue Mountain, then run right back inside, straight through the place and out the rear exit.

And even if he did figure it out, Kevin, who worked the desk, would never tell. Not after the way she imagined Joe had treated him, to get to her.

So, with luck, she had maybe a fifteen minute head start. More than enough, she thought as she reached the corner.

The fog wasn't as dense here. She stepped off the curb, peered in both directions. Hallelujah! The standard joke was that taxis never turned up when you most needed them, but there was a cab coming towards her right now.

Lucy jumped forward and waved her hand wildly. A horn blared, somebody yelled something uncomplimentary, but the taxi swerved towards her and stopped.

The cabbie—a woman—shot her an annoyed look as she opened the door and got inside.

"You feeling suicidal, or what?"

"Or what," Lucy said. She opened her purse and dug inside.

Miss Robinson had insisted on reimbursing her for the things she'd bought, and on paying her for her time, before the party started.

Thank goodness for small favors.

"A bonus if you get me to Pacific Heights ASAP," she said, holding up some bills.

The lady cabbie looked in the mirror. "The fog is going to be a problem."

"So is the man I'm trying to get away from."

That brought a smile to the driver's face. "They're all problems," she said. "Tell you what. I'll do the best I can. Okay?"

Lucy sat back. "That's all anybody can ever ask."

True enough. Doing your best was the most a person could hope for.

Her mouth trembled.

The trouble was that Joe Romano's best wasn't sufficient.

It was bad enough that he thought she was the sort of woman who'd strip at private parties. It was worse that he didn't believe her denials, or trust her. That he really thought she could lie in his arms at night, live with him, share his life…

Who was she kidding?

She didn't share his life. His bed, definitely. His day-to-day existence, sure. But his life?

Mistresses didn't share men's lives. And that was all she was.

Yes, Joe had told her he loved her. It didn't mean anything. He'd been trying to squirm out of what he'd said when he'd come bursting into the café. The odds were good he'd have told her just about anything to make himself look less foolish.

Love? Love was just a word to him. But it was more than that to her. She *loved* him. Really loved him. And there wasn't a way in the world they could reconcile their differences.

Tears rose in Lucy's eyes.

She'd been such a fool. What had become of her common sense? Her morals? Her sense of self?

The cab jerked to a stop.

"We're here," the cabbie said.

Why had she stayed in Joe's house? Slept in his bed? She wasn't stupid.

"Lady? Isn't this what you wanted?"

Lucy's head came up. "No," she said shakily, "no, it's not. What I wanted was for him to love me. That was why I stayed, because I hoped—oh, I really hoped..."

She blinked, met the cabbie's sympathetic look in the mirror.

"Pacific Heights," the cabbie said with surprising gentleness. "This is the address you gave me, right?"

Lucy looked out the window. "Yes," she said, and opened the door of the taxi.

"Lady?"

Lucy looked around.

The cabbie smiled. "You just remember, okay? No guy is worth the sleepless nights or the agony."

"Absolutely," Lucy answered, and told her foolish heart not to argue with such indisputable logic.

She glanced at her watch as she unlocked the front door. With luck, Joe was still driving up and down the streets near the café.

Just in case, though, she bolted all the doors.

Five minutes, she thought as she ran up the stairs, that was all she needed to pack.

It took less than that.

A few seconds to drag her suitcase from the closet and dump it on the bed. Another few to empty the drawers, toss their contents on the carpet. Ditto for the closet; just strip things off the hangers, let them fall. Now it was easy enough to gather everything up, carry it to the bed and hurl it into the suitcase. One armload. Two. And she was—

"Going somewhere, Blondie?"

Lucy cried out, spun around—and saw a narrow-eyed, angry-as-hell Joseph Romano standing in the doorway.

"The doors were locked," she said. "Bolted. Chained. How..."

Joe's mouth curled in a tight smile. "I busted a window."

Her eyes rounded. "You broke a window?"

"That's what I said."

Joe was torn between crossing the room, grabbing Lucy and shaking her until her teeth rattled. Or kissing her until her knees buckled. Or doing both. The last half hour had been hell. He'd envisioned her trapped on a bus that had wrecked in the fog. On a cable car that was out of control, heading full-tilt for the Bay.

Even worse, he'd imagined her standing on the San Francisco side of the Golden Gate Bridge, her mouth set the way it was now, her thumb pointed straight up in the air while a maniac with knives for hands pulled over and asked her if she wanted a lift.

But she was safe, inside his very own house, which was just where he wanted her. He told himself that the thing to do was calm down, act cool, if only for a little while. So he leaned against the doorjamb and folded his arms over his chest.

"What's the problem, Lucinda? Don't guys bust windows in the world you come from?"

"Not unless they're deranged."

"Deranged is a good word. It might just describe the state I'm in, having my woman run out on me that way."

Lucy drew herself up. "I am not your woman, Romano."

"I didn't know where you'd gone."

"That was the general idea."

"Or what had happened to you."

"You want a play-by-play? I took a taxi. I climbed the stairs. I packed."

"You left out the part where you locked all the doors."

"You could have rung the bell."

"Oh, sure. And you'd have come straight to the door and let me in." A cold smile tilted at the corner of Joe's mouth. "You expect me to believe that?"

Lucy looked at him. He was keeping himself in tight control but he couldn't fool her. He was angry. Furious. Well, why wouldn't he be? She was running out on him, he'd just said so. And she bet her life that no woman had ever walked out on Joe Romano before...

Or ever wanted to.

She didn't want to, either. What she wanted, more than anything, was to go into his arms, tell him that she loved him, always would love him...

She swung away, grabbed the suitcase, and heard Joe's footsteps coming up, fast, behind her.

"Put that down, Blondie."

Lucy shook her head. "Just get out of my way, Joe. There's no point in making a scene. It won't change anything."

His hands settled on her shoulders. "Put it down, turn around and look at me."

"No."

"Lucinda."

Her name sounded like music on his lips. She closed her eyes and told herself she was doing the right thing. Joe wanted a toy. He was no different than her father. And she was no different than her father's mistress.

How stupid she'd been, telling herself she was more than a plaything to Joe, just because she wouldn't accept his money.

"Joe." She took a deep breath. "Joe, it's better this way."

"For who?" he said gruffly, and turned her towards him. His eyes, dark with some emotion she was afraid to believe, locked on hers. "Not for me."

"I'm not coming back to you," she said, and tried to keep her voice from quavering. "I was wrong to have stayed with you."

"I want you, Lucy." His voice was soft, almost tender. "I want you to stay with me."

"That's what you think now, Joe. But in a week. A month. A year—"

"Dammit," he said without any anger at all, "will you stop telling me what I think?"

"Joe." Lucy swept the tip of her tongue over her lips. "I'm sorry. I told you I wouldn't be your—your kept woman, but I was. I am. I was just fooling myself, saying I wasn't. And—and I can't be. I can't, because—because—"

"Because you're in love with me," he said.

What was the sense in denying it? "If I am," Lucy said, lifting her chin, "it's my problem."

"Dammit, Lucinda!" Joe shook her, just a little. "It's not anybody's problem, because I love you, too."

"You said that. But I understand. I—"

Joe swept her into his arms and kissed her until she was clinging to him.

"You are an impossible woman," he said when he finally drew back. "You *don't* understand, any more than you know what I'm thinking. Sweetheart." His voice gentled. "I love you, Lucinda Barry. I adore you. I'm not going to live my life without you."

Lucy's eyes locked on his. She wanted to believe him, oh, she wanted to...

"Sweetheart." Joe took a breath. "Will you marry me?"

Her mouth opened, then closed. He laughed and leaned his forehead against hers.

"I never thought I'd see it happen. My Lucinda, speechless."

"Oh, Joe." Tears glittered in Lucy's eyes. "I love you so much..."

He put his hand under her chin, gently raised her face to his. "Then say you'll be my wife. My love, my only love, for the rest of time."

"Yes," Lucy whispered. She laughed, even as the tears spilled down her face. "I will, my darling Joe. I will, I will."

Joe drew her close and kissed her. "You never lied to me. In my heart, I knew that, all along."

She sighed and laid her head against his chest. "Never."

"I even knew you'd never been with another man," he said gruffly. "I just wouldn't admit it, not even to myself." He stroked his hand over her hair and she closed her eyes with pleasure. "The thing was, you scared me out of my skin, honey."

Lucy drew back. "*I* scared *you?*" she said in disbelief.

"Uh-huh." Joe kissed her again. Her lips clung to his, and her hands stole up his chest. "It's not every day a guy falls head over heels in love." He took her hands in his, pressed kisses into the palms. "I want you to know something, honey. Even if those things had been true, even if I hadn't been the

first..." He took a deep breath. "I'd love you, anyway,
Lucinda. Because you're a part of me."

Lucy leaned back in Joe's embrace, smiled, and looped her
arms around his neck.

"I'll probably never be much of a cook."

Joe grinned. "We'll live on coconut-chocolate pom-poms,
and *blini* filled with whipped cream."

"Mmm. The basic food groups. Sounds fine to me."

His smile tilted. "How do you feel about short engage-
ments?"

Lucy laughed softly. "I think they're the very best kind."

Joe swung her into his arms and kissed her. Still kissing her,
he carried her up the stairs.

It was a hot July afternoon, but a cooling breeze fanned the
patio behind Joe Romano's Pacific Heights home throughout
the wedding ceremony and the reception.

Lucy stood in the center of Joe's bedroom, and looked at
herself in the mirror.

"Mrs. Joseph Romano," she whispered, and smiled.

Her gaze went to the terrace windows, and her smile broadened. The guests were all gone now. Lucy's mother and step-
father, Miss Robinson, Matthew and Susannah...

Almost all gone.

Nonna Romano was still on the patio, in earnest conversation with Joe, who had his arm around her.

Lucy looked in the mirror again. She was wearing Nonna's
wedding gown.

Nonna had smiled when they'd told her they were getting
married—after Joe spent half an hour explaining that Lucy
didn't entertain men at parties.

"But is your Lucinda truly not Italian?" Nonna had finally
asked, and Joe had sighed and said that truly, she was not.

"And she cannot cook?"

"No," Joe had replied, putting his arm around Lucy. "But
she loves me, and I love her, and that's all that matters."

Nonna had smiled. "In that case, Joseph, go up to the attic
and find the big white box that holds my wedding gown."

"Uh, it's very sweet of you, darling," Joe had started to say, "but—"

"It's wonderful," Lucy had said. "And I'd be honored to wear it, Mrs. Romano."

"Call me Nonna," Nonna had replied, and then she'd shot Joe a cool look. "What's the matter, Joseph? You think my wedding dress will be too big for your bride? I was not always this size."

"No," Joe had said quickly, "no, of course not..."

Lucy smiled at her reflection and ran her hand down the gently flared skirt of the gown.

Nonna must have been just about her size when she married Joe's grandfather. But she couldn't possibly have been this happy, or this deeply in love. No one could have been. No one ever would be. What she and Joe shared, what they felt for each other...

There was a soft rap at the door.

Lucy turned around. "Come in."

The door opened and her husband—her handsome, wonderful husband—stepped into the room.

"Hi," he said softly.

Lucy smiled. "Hi, yourself."

Joe closed the door behind him. "I'm sorry it took so long, but Nonna—"

"No, that's fine. I'm sure it's not easy for Nonna to think of sharing her favorite grandson with—" Lucy's brows lifted. "What's funny?"

"I wasn't comforting the old witch," he said, "I was hearing her confession."

"Her what?"

He grinned as he undid his tie and tossed it aside. "We've been had, Blondie."

Lucy put her hands on her hips. "I told you not to call me that anymore," she said, trying for, and failing, to sound insulted. Actually, she loved it when Joe called her "Blondie." It reminded her of that first kiss, that first wicked kiss. "What confession?"

"It was all a setup." Joe shrugged off the jacket to his tux, tossed it on a chair and began undoing the studs in his pleated white shirt. "The old schemer planned everything. Seems she'd figured out that the candidates she'd been lining up for the position of Mrs. Joseph Romano weren't ever going to pass scrutiny." The studs gone, he peeled off his shirt and tossed it after the jacket. "She says she interviewed a dozen women before selecting you."

Lucy forced her attention away from her husband's gorgeous, tanned, muscled chest.

"A dozen women," she said, and cleared her throat.

"Which probably means closer to two dozen." Joe undid his belt, opened the button at the top of his fly. "She'd drawn up this profile. Well, of course, she didn't call it that."

"Of course," Lucy echoed as he toed off his shoes and socks. She could be cool about this, if he was, even though they hadn't made love in the month since he'd asked her to marry him. But they'd slept together each night, she nestled in his arms, aware of his heat, of his hard body...

Joe's smile was slow and sexy as he came towards her.

"She decided I needed a woman who was beautiful."

Lucy's heart kicked as he took off her bridal veil.

"And bright."

He turned her so that her back was to him. One by one, she felt the brush of his fingers at the long line of tiny, satin-covered buttons that went from her gown's neckline to its waist.

"A woman who could stand up to me and not back down," he said, his voice just a little hoarse. He pressed his open mouth to her bare shoulder as the gown slipped down, and she caught her breath. "And who was incredibly sexy."

Lucy spun around in his arms. "Your nonna never told you that!"

Joe grinned. "No." His smile tilted. "But you are, you know, Mrs. Romano."

"Are what?" she said softly, and wound her arms around his neck.

"Incredibly, deliciously, magnificently sexy."

Lucy laughed as her husband lifted her in his arms.

"You're just trying to get into my good graces," she said. "You want me to say I'll let you feast on that special dessert, made of angel food cake, whipped cream and melted chocolate."

Joe kissed her until she was breathless.

"Forget the cake," he whispered, and carried his bride to their bed.

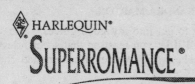

HARLEQUIN
SUPERROMANCE®

You are now entering

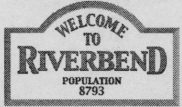

WELCOME TO RIVERBEND
POPULATION 8793

Riverbend...the kind of place where everyone knows
your name—and your business. Riverbend...home of
the River Rats—a group of small-town sons and
daughters who've been friends since high school.

The Rats are all grown up now. Living their lives and
learning that some days are good and some days
aren't—and that you can get through anything
as long as you have your friends.

Starting in July 2000, Harlequin Superromance brings
you Riverbend—six books about the River Rats and
the Midwest town they live in.

BIRTHRIGHT by Judith Arnold (July 2000)
THAT SUMMER THING by Pamela Bauer (August 2000)
HOMECOMING by Laura Abbot (September 2000)
LAST-MINUTE MARRIAGE by Marisa Carroll (October 2000)
A CHRISTMAS LEGACY by Kathryn Shay (November 2000)

Available wherever Harlequin books are sold.

HARLEQUIN®
Makes any time special™

Visit us at www.eHarlequin.com   HSRIVER

If you enjoyed what you just read,
then we've got an offer you can't resist!

Take 2 bestselling love stories FREE!

Plus get a FREE surprise gift!

Coming Next Month

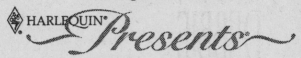

THE BEST HAS JUST GOTTEN BETTER!

#2121 THE ITALIAN'S REVENGE Michelle Reid
Vito Giordani had never forgiven Catherine for leaving, and
now, seizing the advantage, he demanded that she return to
Naples with him—as his wife. Their son would have his parents
back together—and Vito would finally have…revenge!

#2122 THE PLEASURE KING'S BRIDE Emma Darcy
Fleeing from a dangerous situation, Christabel Valdez can't
afford to fall in love. But she can't resist one night of passion
with Jared King. And will one night be enough…?

#2123 HIS SECRETARY BRIDE
Kim Lawrence and Cathy Williams
(2-in-1 anthology)
From boardroom…to bedroom. What should you do if your
boss is a gorgeous, sexy man and you simply can't resist him?
Find out in these two lively, emotional short stories by talented
rising stars Kim Lawrence and Cathy Williams.

#2124 OUTBACK MISTRESS Lindsay Armstrong
Ben had an accident on Olivia's property and had briefly lost
his memory. Olivia couldn't deny the chemistry between them—
but two vital discoveries turned her against him….

#2125 THE UNMARRIED FATHER Kathryn Ross
Melissa had agreed to pose as Mac's partner to help him secure
a business contract. But after spending time with him and his
adorable baby daughter, Melissa wished their deception could
turn into reality….

#2126 RHYS'S REDEMPTION Anne McAllister
Rhys Wolfe would never risk his heart again. He cared about
Mariah, but they were simply good friends. Their one night of
passion had been a mistake. Only, now Mariah was pregnant—
and Rhys had just nine months to learn to trust in love again.

CNM0700